AF478695

VIEWPOINT

VIEWPOINT

by Ben Bova

A Boskone Book
The NESFA Press
Cambridge, Massachusetts
1977

ISBN # 0-915368-14-5   Finebound ISBN # 0-915368-79-X

This edition is limited to 800 numbered copies

This is copy number 134

Table of Contents

This Isn't Exactly
the Way I Had Planned It ..

When I was in high school, I decided to become a chemical engineer. But I wound up in journalism school.

When I got my first job as a newspaper reporter, I figured newspapering was the career for me. So I became a technical editor for an aircraft company.

When I was technically editing on the Vanguard artificial satellite project, I knew that nothing could ever take me away from the space program. A couple of months after we orbited the first Vanguard satellite, I started to write teaching films about high school physics . . . in Watertown, Massachusetts, of all places.

After a couple of years of hobnobbing with the MIT physics faculty, I *knew* that teaching was not the place for me. I had seen my first novel published by then, and decided that I'd be a consultant to industry and a freelance novelist. That's when I took a fulltime job as a science writer for a research laboratory.

Although my laboratory job kept me quite busy, I still made time to write. I met Isaac Asimov. I became a contributor to science fiction magazines. I was a science fiction pro. And then came the first Boskone.

I wrote more and more. I attended more science fiction conventions. I was invited to a Milford Conference, back in the days when they actually *were* in Milford. I met Gordie Dickson. I got a liver transplant.

My career as an aerospace executive soared. I became the first marketing manager in the history of the laboratory. I dabbled in lasers, artificial hearts, superconducting magnets, plasma physics. I met Hans Bethe, Jerome Wiesner, Carl Sagan, Thomas Gold, Edward Teller, Anthony Lewis and other Big Name Scientists. Somehow, I became the editor of a science fiction magazine.

Now I'm the Guest of Honor at a Boskone. This isn't exactly the way I had planned my life . . . but it's been a helluva lot of fun!

Ben Bova
Manhattan
June 1976

Inside Analog
or How I Learned To Stop
Worrying and Love My Job

NESFAns are a very tricky breed. First they inveigle you into fandom by being friendly, throwing parties, running Boskones and an occasional Noreascon, etc. Then they flatter you enormously by asking you to be Guest of Honor at a Boskone. Then they subtly tell you, "Oh, by the way, you'll have to produce a book for the convention, you know."

A book?

"We thought you might want to put together some of your Editorials from *Analog* . . ."

Ah, great: I don't have to do any *real* work.

". . . and maybe answer a few questions we have about how things are done inside the *Analog* office."

With this comes three pages of single-spaced queries, obviously the kind of questions that Archibald Cox had left over when he suddenly found himself unemployed in Washington, D.C. The questions, upon careful examination, fell into several major categories, the first of which dealt with editorial policy:

1. *How much do you let Condé Nast influence your editing of* Analog?

Hardly at all. Condé Nast's attitude is very enlightened. They feel that as long as the magazine makes a profit they should let the Editor do his thing. The only scuffle I ever had was shortly after I started the job, when several shocked readers wrote in to complain about the s-x in "The Gold at the Starbow's End" and "Hero." When I told the company's president that the bra ads in *Made-*

moiselle were much more suggestive than any *Analog* story, he began to shake and asked me to leave his office. He retired the following year.

2. *How much do you let your knowledge of the consumer affect your editing?*

A lot. I'd be silly to put a Sword & Sorcery novelet into *Analog.* Most of our readers detest such stuff, and the ones who do like it know where they can find it. They expect *Analog*-type *science* fiction in *Analog.* Similarly, we don't publish *Star Trek* stories, true love romances, or the kinds of SF that don't deal with science. In a typical *Analog* story, the scientific or technical aspect of the tale is integral to the plot; take it away and the story collapses.

3. *Do you have different criteria for novels than for shorter fiction?*

Not really, although since we can only serialize two to four novels per year, we are constantly overstocked with novels and usually understocked on good short fiction. (Aspiring writers, please take notice!)

4. *Are science articles normally commissioned, or do they come in unsolicited?*

In a few cases I've asked specific writers for specific articles on specific topics. Generally, though, the science articles come in unsolicited. I like to get a query with an outline first, mainly because many articles come in on subjects that we've already covered. Incidentally, science articles for *Analog* should be future-oriented. That is, we don't merely want to know what's being done at the frontiers of research; we want to know what the future implications of such research might be.

5. *What makes you write an in-depth rejection letter on a story?*

Let's face it, no matter how guilty I feel about it, I simply can't write a personal letter about every manuscript I read. If a story is *almost* good enough to buy, I'll write a letter to the author explaining where the problems are, and suggesting how to improve the story. In some cases, I simply want to encourage the author to write another story, even though I can't use the one he or she has submitted. Otherwise, it's either a form letter or a rejection slip.

6. *How many unsolicited manuscripts generally come in per month? Are all the manuscripts read? By whom?*

We get between 200 and 500 manuscripts per month. I read them all, although I must confess some of them get riffled through very quickly. Most of them are very short, thank God.

7. *Why don't you charge to read submissions?*

Because I get paid by Condé Nast to do that. Some editors are not paid by their publishers.

8. *What stories have you seen a million times, and don't ever want to read again?*

I'm sure it hasn't been a million times yet (although it seems that way), but I do get an awful lot of stories that are rewrites of Biblical tales: Adam and Eve, Noah, the Crucifixion, the Second Coming, the Apocalypse. It's very tough to improve on the King James version. Then there's the "tomato surprise" kind of story, in which it turns out that the strange planet being studied by the astronauts is called Earth, or the explosion of the hero's starship is seen in a town called Bethlehem as a new and wondrous star. But since a good writer can made an editor accept any theme, I won't say that I don't want to see stories based on these ideas. Just make them fresh!

9. *How much space in any given issue can you safely risk to touchy or controversial material?*

One hundred percent. *Analog* is an arena of ideas, and it is the Editor's function to keep the readers agitated.

10. *Who writes the blurbs before the stories? Why are they written?*

I write the blurbs. Their purpose is to give the reader a hint of the story's theme: a sort of appetizer that will whet the reader's appetite for the main course.

11. *Do you prefer queries before seeing a manuscript?*

On science articles and novels, yes. Otherwise, no. A query or synopsis of a short story or novelet is almost meaningless, since it's the writing style and characterization that determine the story's salability, more so than the plot.

12. *Some people think it takes a long time for a short-short to come to print. Does it? Why?*

Every issue is built around: (a) the cover story, (b) the novel installment, if any, (c) the science article, and (d) the readers' departments. Short stories are put in as space permits, and picked to either complement or balance the tone of the other pieces. The shorter the story, the more it's likely to be shunted around from month to month until exactly the right "hole" is found for it. Also, the longer the lead stories and novel serializations, the less room we have for shorter pieces.

13. *How often does a novel come to you for serialization with book publication already planned and what is the average holdup when publication isn't already planned?*

Most established writers don't start work on a novel until they have a contract from a book publisher; the contract always specifies a deadline for the mansucript and a planned publication date for the novel. Consequently, almost every novel manuscript we receive from "name" writers already has a book-publication date attached to it. Often this date is too close for us to serialize the novel, since we can only handle two to four novels per year. Occasionally, the writer will sell serialization rights before getting a book publisher to accept the novel; in those cases, we have never delayed the book's publication date by more than a few months.

4

14. *Have there been any Hugo winners which you rejected for publication in* Analog?

I don't remember any, but I do recall that I turned down Fritz Leiber's Nebula-winner, "Catch That Zeppelin," because it was more of a fantasy than a science fiction story.

15. *Do you ever buy material you don't like? Why?*

No. I don't have space enough in the magazine for all the material I *do* like.

16. *Why don't you run record and/or movie reviews?*

Until recently, there hasn't been enough good SF on records or in movies to warrant reviews in *Analog.* We are chronically short of space to publish all the goodies we have on hand, remember. However, we will do occasional pieces on visual and audio media, especially now that *Analog* may be getting into the record business. Our first record is a dramatic presentation of Isaac Asimov's *Nightfall,* with comments by the author at the end of the play. See *Analog* magazine for details on how to obtain this and subsequent *Analog* Records.

17. *Do you have it in for the Art Director?*

I'm not sure what prompted the question, but Herb Stoltz, our Art Director, is one of the best in the business, and a marvelous man to work with. He's responsible for the "look" of *Analog,* and even the illustrators like and respect him—a very unusual state of affairs in the publishing business, let me assure you.

18. *For interior illustrations, how do you pick the artists?*

First, by intuition; you get to know which artist can handle the subject matter of a particular story. Second, by availability; one artist may be overloaded with assignments while another is relatively free.

19. *Do you ever use unsolicited art? Do you commission stories based on artwork?*

No to both questions. And we find it impossible to work with illustrators who can't get into the office for face-to-face discussions on a day's notice.

The next group of questions dealt with my personal ways and attitudes:

20. *Where do you keep your Hugos?*

The Hugos awarded to me personally as Best Professional Editor occupy a place of honor in my Manhattan apartment, just over my wine rack. The earlier Hugos that were awarded to the magazine (i.e., to John W. Campbell, Jr.) were in the office when I arrived on the job and are going to remain there.

21. *How many marshmallows can you throw in a finite amount of time? (For the uninitiated, marshmallow throwing is a required skill for NESFAns.)*

Not enough. But I think we've all found that marshmallow fights are enormously therapeutic. I recommend them to the United Nations without reservation.

22. *Do you let yourself be influenced by what you feel John Campbell would have done?*

No way. Nobody on God's green earth could do things the way John did, and it would be silly to try.

23. *Now that you read constantly for* Analog, *do you ever read for fun? Do you read science journals?*

I don't do as much "fun" reading as I'd like to, but here and there I sneak in something that's neither science nor science fiction. I regularly read *Scientific American, New Scientist, Science News,* and *Science* magazines. And *Locus,* of course.

6

24. *When are we going to read more fiction from Ben Bova? Have you ever, or will you ever, publish your own stories in* Analog?

If you can't find fiction by Ben Bova, you're just not looking in the right places. In 1976, Random House published *Millennium*, Scribner's published *City of Darkness* (dedicated to NESFAns), and Bobbs-Merrill published *The Multiple Man*. All are hardcover novels. The same year, Pyramid brought out the paperback version of *The Starcrossed*. I will not publish any fiction in *Analog*, under my own name or a pseudonym, nor will I submit any stories to any other science fiction magazine.

25. *How do you use your time?*

Generally, I spend Tuesdays through Thursdays in the *Analog* office, and try to save the other four days of the week for my own writing and personal affairs. The manuscripts that don't get read Tuesday through Thursday, however, are read during the Friday through Monday period. I hate to let manuscripts sit around unread. This has sometimes caused stunned writers to complain that I couldn't possibly be reading their stories so quickly. They never have that complaint when a story's bought, however.

26. *How many conventions per year do you attend?*

Regularly: Boskone, Minicon, and the WorldCon. Sometimes: Philcon. Once: a Lunacon and the first Mexicon. Also, all those at which I am Guest of Honor.

The remaining questions dealt with reader reactions to *Analog*, circulation matters, office routine, and general science fiction topics:

27. *Do you get letters complaining of obscenity in the stories you publish?*

Of course. But we get more complaints about mathematical slipups, or incorrect dialects of foreign languages.

28. *How long did the $1.00 price tag of* Analog *affect its sales?*

It still is, although I believe it's a combination of increased cover price and decreased loose change in our readers' pockets that have caused a slump in newsstand sales. We were averaging 70,000 newsstand sales per month in 1972 and haven't quite come back up to that standard. On the other hand, subscriptions continue to increase; they now represent just about 40% of our total sales.

29. *What motivations affect your planning of special topic issues?*

Circulation, firstly. Fun, for the Editor and the readers, secondly.

30. *Does the circulation of other SF magazines affect* Analog?

Slightly. When circulation dips for one magazine in this field, it seems to dip for everyone to some degree. I would welcome several strong SF magazines to the newsstands; they would reinforce our sales, I think, rather than compete with them.

31. *How many people are involved in putting out* Analog, *from first readers to final printing?*

I am the first reader. Victoria Schochet and her assistant do all the production work, once I've bought the manuscripts. Herb Stoltz does the layouts. I assign the artwork, and Herb and I come to an agreement on each piece. Our Circulation Manager gets into the act on the cover illustrations, making our normal three-ring circus into a four-ring circus. However, in case of a tie, the Editor wins. I don't know how many people are involved in printing *Analog*; that work is done at Rumford Press, in New Hampshire.

32. *How many letters generally come in per month?*

I've never counted them, but I get the feeling it's rather consistent with the number of manuscripts—from fifty to a hundred per week. Our policy is to answer personally all the letters that don't get into the Brass Tacks column.

33. *How about the possibilities of* Analog *books, such as* Analog Annual*? What will affect their future?*

   Analog Annual was an experiment in doing a "thirteenth issue" of the magazine that would capture the paperback readers who don't normally buy magazines. If its sales are good, we will do more. I'd also like to do some anthologies based on the classic *Astounding* stories, and revive *Unknown Worlds* as a quarterly paperback.

34. *Do you think science fiction will degenerate with its newfound popularity?*

   A lot of things called science fiction will degenerate and ultimately blow away, especially the vapid movies and television shows that are currently getting so much publicity. This is nothing new, and I don't think it will affect the "hard core" of science fiction. If anything, it should attract a few new level-headed and loyal fans to the field. On the other hand, science fiction will not become the mass-media darling that some prophets believe it will be, simply because the masses do not care to do the thinking that science fiction demands of them.

35. *Is the sense of wonder dying in this technical age?*

   I believe that question was first asked by Cardinal Bramante to Galileo. The answer was "no" then, and it's still "no" today. Look at the enthusiastic public response to the Viking pictures from Mars, or to Gerard O'Neill's concept of L-5 space colonies.

36. *Why don't you advertise cigarettes?*

   For the same reason I don't advertise handguns. They may be soothing to some people, but they are killers. I may be forced to advertise cigarettes and other things I don't particularly like, though, if our costs for paper, ink, and postal services continue to rise as steeply as they have been.

37. *Have you heard from Kelvin Throop lately?*

No, but he's a very surprising fellow and might pop up at any time—maybe at a WorldCon costume competition.

38. *Why don't you attend NESFA meetings any more?*

I'd really like to, but the New York subways stop somewhere in the Bronx, and the Boston subway system apparently doesn't go that far south. Why don't you hold a NESFA meeting in New York? Sundays are usually very quiet, and we could start the meeting with a cheap but good champagne brunch down in my neighborhood.

The Mystic West

Everybody talks about "the Two Cultures" but nobody does anything about it. Except science fiction people! Even before C.P. Snow enunciated the Two Cultures split between science and the humanities, scholars such as Robert Graves and Malcolm Muggeridge were decrying the "dehumanization" of western civilization by science and technology. Graves's little diatribe in the British journal *New Scientist* triggered this Editorial, in which I tried to show how science fiction bridges the gap between the Two Cultures.

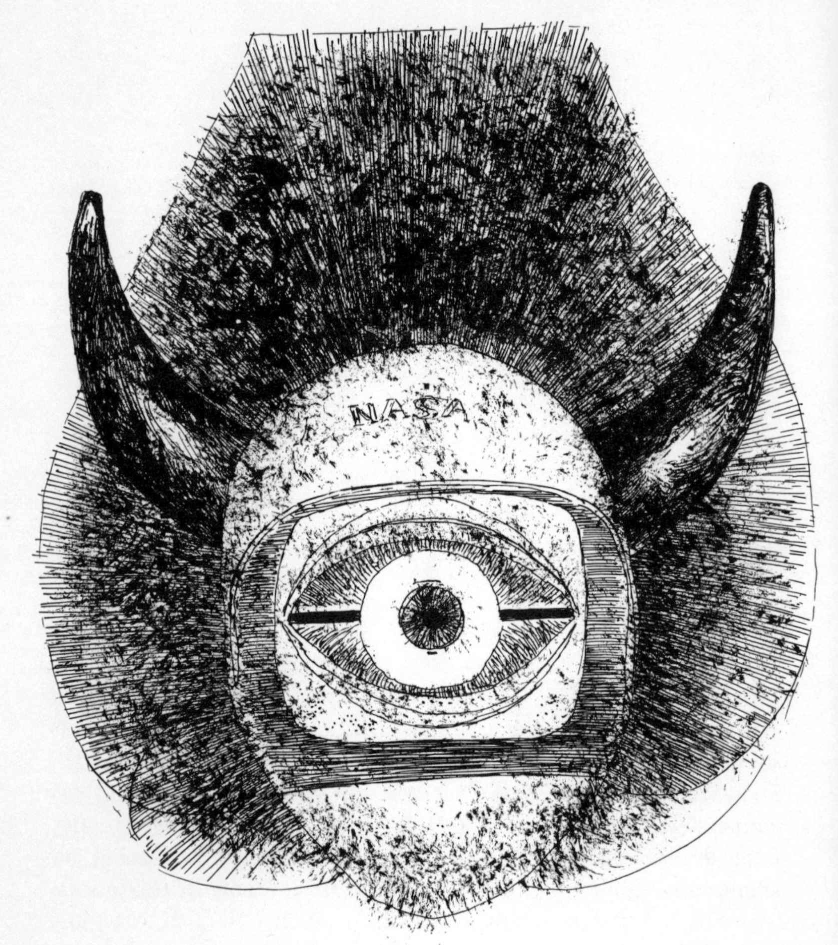
NASA

Writing in the British journal *New Scientist,* the famed poet and historian Robert Graves recently said: "Technology is now warring openly against the crafts, and science covertly against poetry."

What Graves seems to be saying is that technology is allowing machines to replace human muscle power and handiwork—a discovery that the Luddites made nearly two centuries ago. What he doesn't say, but apparently fears, is the possibility that machines, such as electronic computers, might replace human brain power.

Graves's fears about technology are bad enough. Unfounded, maybe, but what the hell. 'Tis the season for pointing quavering fingers at technology and science. His attack on science itself is on a more mystical level, and seems even more unfounded. He contrasts science with poetry, and claims that poetry has a power that scientists can't recognize, "because at its most intense [poetry] works in the Fifth Dimension, independent of time."

He goes on to say that poetry is usually the product of intuitive thinking, and grants that some mathematical theories have also sprung from intuition. Then he says, "Yet scientists would dismiss a similar process . . . as 'illogical'."

Apparently Graves sees scientists as a sober, plodding phalanx of soulless thinking machines, doing everything rationally, never making a step that hasn't been carefully scouted out in advance. He should try working with a few, or even reading *The Double Helix.*

As a historian, Graves ought to be aware that James Clerk Maxwell's brilliant insight about electromagnetism—the guess that visible light is only one small slice of the huge spectrum of electromagnetic energy—was an intuitive leap into the unknown. Maxwell had precious little real evidence to back his guess. It wasn't until Hertz produced radio waves and Roentgen stumbled onto X rays that Maxwell's theoretical predictions were verified. Max Planck's original concept of the quantum theory was also mainly intuition. And the list of wild jumps of intuition made by these supposedly stolid, humorless scientists is long indeed.

It turns out that scientists are just as human, just as intuitive, just as emotional as any of us. But most people don't realize this. *They don't know scientists*, any more than they know science.

As C.P. Snow pointed out decades ago, there is a gap between the Two Cultures, and Graves shows a particularly painful chasm. Graves is a scholar who is widely and justly renowned for his work in ancient mythology, where he's combined his gifts of poetry and historical research in a truly beautiful way.

But he doesn't seem to know scientists, the men and women who do science. That's just as bad—worse, maybe—as not caring to know anything about science itself. And a person who doesn't understand science is simply not well-educated. Not in today's world.

Graves's attack on science gets particularly virulent when he says: "The worst that one can say about modern science is that it lacks a unified conscience, or at least it has been forced to accept the power of Mammon. Mammon . . . exploits the discoveries of science for the benefit of the international financiers, enabling them . . . to control all markets and governments everywhere."

He ends by saying, "There need have been no war between Science and Poetry, nor between Technology and the Arts, had not the power of money forced too many poor, married scientists and technologists to break what should have been a Hippocratic oath to use their skills only for the benefit of mankind."

That's a serious charge, made all the more serious by Graves's undoubted stature as a scholar. It points out problems that go far beyond the work of the scientists themselves. What significant group of people in the world today has "a unified conscience"? Do "international financiers" really control most national governments? How can scientists—or poets, or plumbers—determine what is "the benefit of mankind"?

It's significant that Graves ends up by attacking not science itself, but the *uses* to which science is put: the interface between scientific research and political policies, between the laboratory and the market place.

If this is where the problem is, why blame only the scientist? What part of the responsibility belongs to the politician and industrialist? To the taxpayer and the poet? After all, all that a scientist wants to do—as a scientist—is the research that interests him. But the world isn't that kind to anyone. A scientist can only get to do the research that somebody will pay for.

Since the earliest flickerings of scientific curiosity, more than a hundred centuries ago, the scientist had to justify his existence. Why should a king support someone who does no useful work? The farmers produce food, the soldiers protect the kingdom or enlarge it, the tax-gatherers ... well, everybody knows what they do. Why support a stargazer?

It turned out that the stargazers had some practical help to give. They could make calendars and predict the seasons—a very important trick in an agricultural society. And since they showed that the patterns of the stars affected events here on Earth, such as seasons, it was only a short step to astrology—predicting the affairs of individual people by the positions of the stars.

Astrology became a rooted part of astronomy for many long centuries. Galileo and Kepler cast horoscopes. Kings and emperors kept astronomers about them for their astrological predictions, not their studies of the universe. The *astronomical* went on, but only because the astrological forecasts were in demand.

Even today, the scientist still must pay his "astrological" dues to his patron. They're no longer casting horoscopes but their patrons still exact the same kind of payment. For example, a physics student looking for a research position in almost any nation on Earth has a much easier time finding funds if he works on a defense-related project.

Major astronomical installations have been built *first* because they could help the military watch potential enemies better, and only secondly because they might be useful in unraveling the mysteries of the universe. Chemists and biologists, for many years, found it easier to get funding in chemical and biological warfare programs than in public health research.

If it's the fault of the scientists for letting themselves be used in this way, it's equally the fault of the tax-paying public for insisting on strong military defense programs. Vietnam has drastically changed the mood of most Americans toward the military. But hardly anyone really wants us to disarm completely. And at this point in history, scientific research is a vital part of military power.

There's an old poolroom saying, "Put your money where your mouth is." Despite the loud noises being made in Washington and elsewhere about beating swords into plowshares and using our scientific and technological know-how to solve "the problems of the people," we are still spending more on military research and development than on all other forms of government-sponsored R&D. The Pentagon's R&D budget is about eight billion dollars. That's just about as much as all the other government agencies—from Health to NASA—have *in total.*

A scientist who wants to do research in his chosen field will almost inevitably be drawn into a defense-related program, unless his field is completely outside the Pentagon's areas of interest. You can't do research on promises, or political speeches. You need equipment and assistants. You need money. The Pentagon gets the money and calls the tune. If the tune is to be changed, it *can't* be by the scientists alone. It must be by the taxpayers, who have the power to decide where their research money should be spent.

Which brings us back to the crux of the problem: the average man doesn't know the scientists.

Since the prehistoric days of tribal shamans, most people have held an ambivalent attitude toward the medicine man-astrologer-wizard-scientist. On the one hand they envied his abilities and sought to use his power for their own gain. On the other hand, they feared his power, hated his seeming superiority, and knew damn well that he was in league with the dark forces of evil.

There's been very little change in that double-edged attitude over the centuries. Today we still tend to hold the scientists in awe. After all, they're the ones who brought us nuclear power, modern medicines, space flight, and underarm deodorants. Yet at the same time we also see scientists derided as fuzzy-brained eggheads or coldly ruthless, emotionless makers of monsters.

Scientists are a minority group, and like most minority groups, they're largely hidden from the public's sight. They're tucked away in ghettos—laboratories, campuses, field sites out in the desert, or on Pacific atolls. Before the public can really understand what science can and cannot do, the people must get to see and understand the scientists themselves. See them as human beings. Get to know their work, their aims, their dreams and their fears.

A possible answer to this problem of humanizing scientists comes from the same field in which Graves has made his biggest contribution: the study of mythology.

Joseph Campbell, Professor of Literature at Sarah Lawrence College, has spent a good deal of his life studying mythology and writing books on the subject, such as the four-volume *The Masks of God* and *Hero with a Thousand Faces*. He has pointed out that modern man has no real mythology to depend on. The old myths are dead, but no new mythology has been raised to take their place.

And man needs a mythology, he insists, to give a sort of emotional meaning to the world in which we live. A mythology is a kind of codification on an emotional level of man's attitudes toward life, death, and the whole vast, sometimes scarifying universe.

An example. Almost every primitive culture has a Prometheus legend. In our western culture, the Greek version is the one most quoted. Prometheus was a demigod who saw man as a weak, starving, freezing creature, barely surviving among the animals of the fields and woods. Taking pity on man, Prometheus stole fire from the heavens and gave it to man, at the cost of a horrible punishment to himself. But man, with fire, became master of the Earth and even a challenge to the gods.

A typical myth, fantastic in detail, yet absolutely correct in spirit. One of man's early ancestors "discovered" fire about half a million years ago. Most likely, these primitive *Homo erectus* types saw lightning turn shrubbery into flame: hence the legend of the gift from the heavens. Before fire, our primitive ancestors were just another marginal anthropoid. With fire, we've become the dominant species on this planet.

The Prometheus myth "explains" this titanic event in terms that simple people can understand and accept. The myth gives an emotional flavoring to the bald facts.

Much of today's emotion-charged, slightly irrational urge toward astrology and spiritualism is really a groping for a new mythology, a mythology that can explain the modern world on an emotional, intuitive level to people who are frightened that they're too small and weak to cope with this universe.

Joseph Campbell's work has shown that there are at least four major functions that any mythology must accomplish.

First: a mythology must induce a feeling of awe and majesty in the people: what science-fictionists call "a sense of wonder."

Second: a mythology must define and uphold a system of the universe, a pattern of self-consistent explanation for the phenomena of the world around us. A modern mythology would have a ready-made system of the universe: the known and continuously-expanding body of knowledge that we call science.

Third: a mythology usually supports the social establishment. For example, what we today call ancient Greek mythology apparently originated with the Achaean conquerors of the earlier Mycenaean civilization. Zeus was a barbarian sky god who conquered the local goddesses of the Mycenaean cities. Many a lovely legend was started that way.

Fourth: a mythology serves as a crutch to help the individual member of the society through the emotional crises of life, such as the transition from childhood into adulthood, and the inevitability of death.

It just might be that this beloved thing we call science fiction, when it's at its very best, might serve some of these functions of a new mythology.

Certainly science fiction tries to induce a sense of wonder about the physical universe and man's own interior private universe of the mind. Science fiction depends heavily on known scientific understanding as the basic underpinning of a universal order.

Science fiction doesn't tend to support a given political establishment, but does almost invariably back the social bent of western civilization: that is, the concept that the individual man is worth more than the Organization—whatever it may be—and that nothing is more important than human freedom.

Whether or not science fiction serves to help people through emotional crises is more difficult to tell. It's interesting that science fiction has a large readership among the young, the teen-agers who need to find their own individual place in the universe. And how many of our stories about super-heroes and time travel and interstellar flights are really an attempt to deny the inevitability of death?

Nobody intends to certify science fiction as The New Mythology. That's not the intention of either the writers, or the readers. But the beleaguered scientists who are being chivvied by an unsympathetic, know-nothing public might come and sit around our campfire, at least. Maybe we can help each other.

Giant Step Backward

Hell hath no fury like a fundamentalist scorned. This Editorial, with its modest proposal that Genesis is lousy as a biology text, drew more irate letters from readers than any Editorial before or since. One terribly upset lady sent me a Bible in an effort to save my obviously damned soul. An occasional letter still comes in, pointing out my errors and "proving" that Evolution is false because some scientist has just uncovered new evidence that contradicts some other scientist. To each correspondent I made one simple request: give me some piece of physical evidence—as solid as a fossil tooth—that supports the theory of Creationism. To date, no evidence. A lot of letters, but not one scrap of proof. I still prefer Evolution as an explanation for our presence in the Universe. Even though Genesis is better written than most biology texts.

California is a land of contrasts. Stark desert lies next to balmy Riviera-like seashore. Sequoia forests and stony mountains are within easy distance of huge, smog-laden cities. The aerospace industry and the most productive astronomical observatories in the world sit amidst religious fundamentalists and sects of all descriptions.

And in the state-approved biology textbooks for elementary schools, the origin of man is illustrated by a photograph of Michelangelo's Sistine Chapel paintings.

The Sistine Chapel paintings, and the concepts that they illustrate, are powerful, beautiful, and deeply moving. But they are not biology, by any stretch of the imagination. The California Board of Education has bowed to the pressures of religious fundamentalists and other perhaps well-meaning people, and ordained that the Biblical explanation of man's origins, as given in Genesis, shall be taught in the schools as an hypothesis of equal validity with the evolutionary concepts of Charles Darwin and the biologists.

Quite frankly, this is nonsense.

Remember the Scopes Monkey Trial in Tennessee in 1925? Scopes lost. Although he had to pay only a nominal fine, and the anti-evolutionary law became a laughing matter, it wasn't until 1970 (!) that the last anti-evolution law in our fifty states was revoked.

Having lost the battle to prevent the teaching of evolution by legal strictures, the anti-evolutionists have reopened the battle with a subtler approach. They demand that the Genesis explanation for human origins be taught with equal weight as the teaching of evolution. To be logically consistent, they should also insist that the phlogiston theory of combustion, the caloric theory of heat, and the Ptolemaic description of the solar system be taught alongside their modern counterparts. No doubt the Flat Earth Society should have its innings, too. And to be fair, the fundamentalists of other religions should be allowed to get their stories into the biology texts. After all, once we admit the Genesis description, why not cover the whole picture and include the Buddhist, Taoist, Greco-Roman, Norse and all other mythologies? (Fortunately, Genesis covers three of the major world religions: Christianity, Islam, and Hebrew.)

I was raised a Roman Catholic, and exposed very early to the beauty and power of Genesis. But no theologian that I know seriously believes that this account, written several thousand years ago and based on even earlier oral tales, is literally true in the sense that the results of a laboratory experiment are verifiably true. Like all myths, the Genesis story was originally aimed at trying to explain the unexplainable. Today, such myths are important as illustrations of the moral principles by which we attempt to guide our lives. But they are not literally true: the events described in Genesis did not actually take place.

Thomas Aquinas knew that and so, I suspect, does Pope Paul VI. The Catholic Church has accepted evolutionary teaching much in the spirit that Darwin himself first offered it: as an attempt to show how God accomplished His work, not an attempt to overthrow religious belief.

Genesis is not "wrong" or useless. It is merely not biology. The philosophical, religious and historical information content of the Bible is not valid when it comes to teaching biology, any more than the same data are valid when it comes to treating tuberculosis or setting a broken bone.

And the overwhelming weight of evidence in favor of evolution makes me wonder how anyone can doubt the truth of the concept. For more than a century, fossils of early types of pre-human ancestors have been found and categorized. These stony remains of *Proconsul, Australopithecus, Homo erectus,* the Neander-thals and finally *Homo sapiens* show how we slowly evolved from smaller, less brainy creatures. We didn't "descend" or "ascend" from the apes: we evolved with them from common progenitors. The modern-day apes are our cousins, not our grandfathers.

The evidence of modern biology and genetics shows the mechanics of evolution, from Gregor Mendel's studies of heredity, using pea plants, to the molecular understandings of DNA and RNA.

While there are plenty of questions and arguments over the details of evolutionary theory, I know of no serious doubts in any scientist's mind that life on Earth evolved quite naturally out of inert chemicals, and that the human race is one result of this biological sequence.

Why do some people get upset with the idea that human beings are no different, biologically, than any other creature on this planet? In effect, what they are saying is that they want to think of themselves as separate from the rest of creation, "above" the other plants and animals, lord and master of the Earth and all its creatures.

This attitude is certainly not humble. It separates humankind from nature by allowing men to think of themselves as different and somehow better than everything else on Earth. This is the attitude that has led men to think of nature as something to be conquered and used, without caring about the consequences. It is an attitude that can be very useful for a small band of pioneers faced with an untamed and vast frontier. It is an attitude that can be very dangerous for a civilization that is experiencing a planet-wide population boom. It is an anti-ecology attitude that bulldozes apple orchards to make room for housing developments.

People are more important than trees. But in a very real sense, without the trees, without the life-support systems of spaceship Earth, the human race will either die away or migrate. And we're not quite ready to migrate.

The classic Judeo-Christian attitude, as it comes down to us today, is essentially "Man above nature." Interestingly, the Eastern religions strive for a harmony of man with nature. Perhaps this accounts for their growing popularity around the world. On a planet where environmental problems abound, people are beginning to turn toward a system of belief that stresses ecological sanity.

In California, the question of teaching religious mythology in biology classes has been averted by a compromise that, I suspect, pleases no one. Evolution will be taught in the biology classes, and Genesis will be taught in history classes.

This year. But what will be the long-term effects of the fundamentalist attack on science? About one-third of the nation's textbooks are sold in California. Right now, the biology-text publishers are producing a special California edition that includes references to Biblical lore. What if the publishers decide (as publishers often do) that it will be cheaper to print *all* their books one way, and since California insists on including Genesis in its biology texts, the whole nation will get Genesis? What happens if and when the fundamentalists begin to attack in other states, on other subjects?

Man is an explanation-seeker. Many people—including, I suspect, the fundamentalists—find themselves in an incredibly complex society, a world that they can neither understand nor explain to themselves. Therefore they turn to religion for an order, a structure to the universe. The order and structure that science provides doesn't suit them, mainly because science is more difficult to understand, science admits that its answers are only approximations to truth and therefore apt to be changed at an instant's notice, and also because science does not place an all-wise, all-compassionate intelligence at the head of the universe.

Science tells us that the universe is understandable, even though we may never grasp the complete picture. But it is impersonal; there is no benevolent ruler making certain that everything comes out O.K. Most religions tell us that there is an absolute truth and they have it; this truth comes from God, who is personally interested in us, and wants to guide us toward eternal happiness.

And perhaps that's the *real* difference between science and religion: this question of what happens after death. The earliest known religious ceremonies were burials, where primitive hunting tribes—Neanderthal as well as *sapiens*—carefully placed a hunter's tools and weapons in the grave with him, so that he'd be prepared for a continued life. Today, people are beginning to preserve their bodies cryogenically, surrounded by the support systems of modern technology, in preparation for a literal life after death, right here on Earth.

For millennia, religion has been offering a form of life after death. Today, science is beginning to offer the same thing.

But at heart, science has always remained silent on the question of an afterlife. Religion has always used the idea of an afterlife as a carrot and a stick. If you behave well in this life, you will be rewarded with heaven. If not, eternal hell awaits you.

Most modern people claim that they've rejected these ancient religious ideas. Yet the fundamentalists can influence textbook publishers. And the evidence here in the office of *Analog* shows that religious ideas are still very much a part of modern man's psyche.

Every week, writers send to *Analog* stories that "explain" the Creation, the life of Christ, the Flood and other Biblical events. They use science-fiction terms for their explanations: the Star of Bethlehem was actually an exploding interstellar spacecraft; Christ was an extraterrestrial visitor; and so on.

Some powerful stories have come from this. Arthur C. Clarke's "The Star" is the classic example. But there's a curious double twist in such stories. Essentially, the writer is saying that he wants to explain Biblical events in terms of modern science and technology, because he doesn't believe that the Bible properly explains what happened. In other words, God didn't just open a path in the Red Sea for the fleeing Israelites; a team of extraterrestrial engineers decided to help the Jews. Yet the writer is also saying that he believes such an event actually happened, that the mythological tales of the Bible are literally real, and therefore must be explained in terms that a modern person can accept.

Dostoevski's Grand Inquisitor, in *Crime and Punishment*, said that all human beings need "miracle, mystery, and authority." The Bible provides all three, woven together. Science tries to understand the miracles, clear up the mysteries, and make man himself responsible for his own actions—the authority of a god (and the associated authority of the state) is replaced by individual responsibility.

And there we have the crux of the problem. Who is responsible for my actions? Am I a puppet being pulled by heavenly (or hellish) strings? Am I a puppet being cleverly manipulated by behaviorist psychologists or implacable socio-economic forces? Or am I an individual with a range of free action open to me? And if so, how wide is that range?

Most religions ultimately place their god at the center of every human being's behavior: either you walk in the ways of the Lord, or you are damned. In other words, either God is guiding you or the devil is.

Those science-fiction stories that attempt to "explain" the myths of the Bible end up merely by replacing the Bible's well-thought-out structure with other gods: alien races, natural forces, coincidences.

Modern science is showing us that we may not have the total and complete freedom of action that we once thought we did. But still, our range of individual free choice is enormously wide. And the more we know about our physical and psychological limitations, the more we can do about overcoming them. No man can fly to the Moon or even lift himself off the ground by muscle power alone. But when man decided he was meant to fly, he didn't grow wings, he invented aerodynamics and rocketry.

In the subtler fields of ethics and social behavior, we find that man's choice of actions is not truly unlimited. Yet we dare not abandon all responsibility for our actions and behave irrationally. There are names for people who act that way; and places in which to put them.

Down at the core of man's striving for understanding, we have the conflict between the religious and scientific approaches. Religion says all the answers are known and the universe is being run by a superbeing. Science says the answers are largely unknown, but knowable, and it looks like we're on our own.

We learn through the clash of ideas. Both religion and science have much to tell us, and every human being should be free to choose for himself how much weight he gives to each approach.

The frightening thing about the California biology text situation is that it raises the specter of narrow-minded bigotry that always tries to drive competing ideologies out of the society. Scientists have been accused of having just this attitude. But a study of history will show that it's the religious zealots—who are convinced they have *the* answer—who close their minds to all other ideas.

One of the saddest accomplishments of the Roman Catholic Church, once it became the official state religion of the Roman Empire, was to close schools that were not Church supervised. The famous Academy of Athens, seat of the accumulated wisdom of Socrates, Plato, and Aristotle, was shut down. The Dark Ages were not far off.

Could it happen today? With all our vast knowledge and instant electronic communications? Certainly. As one writer put it decades ago, instant communications means that the village idiot can be heard around the world with the speed of light, if you give the village idiot the microphone.

If this kind of thinking has gained a toehold in California schools, it's a giant step backward for American education.

Mental Energy Crisis

At the height of the furor over the Arab oil embargo of late 1973, as I walked to the office one morning and noted how clear the air was (thanks to the smaller number of automobiles fouling the city), I began to think that perhaps we are all looking at the Energy Crisis in the wrong light. And then I wondered what an unreconstructed libertarian like Patrick Henry would say about all the stumbling and mumbling going on in Washington. Nobody talks about the Energy Crisis anymore, but the Looney Tunes policies of our Government stumble right along, proving that the real energy crisis is literally in our heads.

"They tell us, sir, that we are weak ... But when shall we be stronger? Will it be the next week, or the next year?"

Patrick Henry asked that in his renowned "liberty or death" speech in 1775.

There's a curious echo of this question in the current national dither over the energy crisis.

The mood in Washington is very reminiscent of the combination of gloom and panic that was rampant some sixteen years ago, when the Russians launched Sputnik and established an early lead in the so-called Space Race. There was the same dithering, the same pointing of shaking fingers, the same feelings of fright and frustration, the same scary realization that we were in deep trouble in an area that we had always taken for granted.

It's fashionable to believe—now—that the Space Race was an ephemeral creation of politicians and industrial hacks; that the so-called Missile Gap was a public relations maneuver to win votes and hugely profitable contracts for the aerospace companies. Yet the Race was very real. There was a time when the Soviet Union had nuclear-armed missiles standing ready for flight and we had none. That is part of the reason why we never intervened in the Hungarian rebellion of 1956. There was a time when the Russians were far ahead of us in space feats, and used these triumphs to impress the nations of the underdeveloped world. This was the time when the Russians penetrated the Middle East with technical and military assistance programs. The Arabs were rightly impressed by the Sputniks, Luniks, and Vostoks.

There have been loud cries of despair over the current energy crisis, and equally loud grumblings to the effect that the whole thing is an artificially created problem, a manufactured scare produced by the politicians and the big oil companies, who are manipulating us into allowing the oil companies to raise their prices, escape environmental protection rules, and drill for oil everywhere and anywhere they choose to.

What are the facts?

Are we truly in a deep crisis, where we will have to drastically change our energy consumption patterns? Or are we being manipulated by a sinister combination of governmental and industrial Svengalis?

Just as in the wildest days of the early Space Race, the facts are hard to come by. There's a flood of information, claims and counterclaims, but real, verifiable facts seem extremely rare. Let's get back to the very basic areas, and see what we can learn about the situation.

Basically, our energy systems consist of the following components: fuel resources, such as deposits of fossil fuels (coal, oil, gas), fissionables, or other potential fuels; processing facilities, in which the fuels are prepared for use; distribution systems for getting the fuels from their original locations to the processing facilities and then to the users; electric power plants, where some of the fuel is converted into electricity; distribution systems for the electricity; and finally the myriad end uses of the energy—which range from home heating to transportation to electric toothbrushes.

There is no shortage of fuel resources. By every estimate from any source whatever, the conclusion is that there is enough oil to keep feeding world consumption at its present level for at least another century. But most of the known oil deposits are in Arab lands, and the Arabs are using this resource as a weapon in their struggle against Israel.

To a world that has blithely assumed that Arab oil would not only be available indefinitely, but would be available cheaply, the Arab oil embargo has been a devastating shock. The United States, which now consumes between one-quarter and one-third of the entire world's output of energy, and Western Europe, which is the next hungriest energy consumer, have been especially hard hit.

Although the latest phase of the fratricidal Arab-Israeli war triggered the oil embargo, it seems clear that the Arabs would have been raising the prices of their oil sooner or later. Since the end of World War Two, America and Western Europe have been buying oil from the Arabs at prices that were almost literally dirt cheap. It was inevitable that the Arabs would someday realize how dependent we are on their only export item, and start hiking the prices.

What about other sources of fossil fuel? The US is actually fantastically rich in such resources. True, most of our oil and natural gas wells are being rapidly depleted. Even the newly-developed fields in Alaska's North Slope region aren't big enough to satisfy more than a small percentage of our current consumption. But we have vast coal deposits, both in the eastern Appalachian regions and in western states such as Montana, Wyoming and North Dakota. In addition, we have oil shale deposits and offshore oil fields that have not been utilized yet.

In all, conservative estimates show that we have within our own territory fossil fuel deposits that are easily ten times more abundant than all the oil in the Middle East. Enough fossil fuel to keep us going for five hundred years, at least.

But—it's now impossible to use these resources without staggering environmental damage. Stripping the water-scarce western states of their coal deposits could scar those areas permanently. The same would happen if we began digging up the oil shale. And no one really wants offshore oil rigs messing up the beaches where they live or play.

Moreover, much of this fuel—especially the western coal—is high in sulfur. Burning it in power plants, for example, would create serious air pollution problems.

Somewhat the same situation applies to our stores of nuclear fuels, uranium and thorium. We have enough fissionables in our own ground to last not merely for centuries or even a millennium or two; there's enough for a million years, according to most estimates. Even assuming that we don't use breeder reactors to convert low-grade fissionables into high-grade, useful fuel, there's enough uranium easily available for a century or more, at the most conservative estimate.

But again, environmental questions come up. Are nuclear power plants really safe? Can they be operated without creating unacceptable levels of thermal pollution of our water resources?

We have the fuel resources. Whether or not we can use them depends on several factors. It's clear that the big oil companies are using the energy crisis to try to evade the constrictions placed on them a few years ago by an environment-conscious public. The oil companies are saying, in essence, "Let us dig for oil wherever we want to, and stop hampering us with all these frilly considerations of air pollution and environmental degradation, and we'll have everything back to normal pretty soon."

Even if we let them have their way, the one thing that won't be back to normal for a long time (if ever) is the price we must pay for energy.

One of the major reasons for that—and a prime factor in the crisis—is that the United States simply does not have enough oil refining facilities to supply the nation with adequate refined petroleum products.

For decades, the oil companies have consistently "underestimated" the nation's growing demands for oil and its byproducts, and have built refineries at a rate less than the actual growth of demand. This has resulted in our need to import refined oil—we actually ship crude oil overseas and then re-import it (our own oil!) after it's been refined.

So, the oil companies have not spent as much of their capital on refineries as the situation demanded. The result is that petroleum products are scarcer, in greater demand than ever. So the oil companies are "forced" to raise their prices! Their profits, crisis or not, have been rising steadily.

What about new sources of energy? New fuels? There are plenty of good ideas available, from hydrogen as a replacement for the fossil fuels, through geothermal power, solar power, power from the sea, and—ultimately—fusion power. No doubt all of these will come into use, one way or another. We will have hydrogen-fueled cars and planes someday, and solar-heated houses and office buildings. Much of California could be powered by geothermal energy, and many seacoast areas could make use of the ocean's temperature differentials to create electrical energy.

Ultimately we will have thermonuclear fusion, and when that happens our energy crisis will be solved forever.

But all of these bright promises will take a minimum of five to ten years before they become realities.

Let me tell you briefly about one such bright promise. It's a good example of how this entire energy business got into a crisis situation.

In 1959 I went to work for the Avco Everett Research Laboratory, mainly to help publicize their research in a new technique of generating electrical power, called magnetohydro-dynamics (MHD).

At that time, a combination of several electric utility companies and Avco Corporation had decided that the nation's growing demand for electrical energy meant that new and more efficient power generation technology was vitally needed.

It was known then—in 1959!—that the United States' demand for electricity was growing at a rate that doubled the demand every ten years. Forecasters were showing that the standard technology would not be able to keep up with the demand. The goal of the MHD program was to have working MHD power generators on the line in the 1970's.

Without going into details on how an MHD generator works (I wrote an article on the subject that appeared in the May 1965 *Analog*), the main point is that an MHD power plant would be at least fifty percent more efficient than a standard power plant. The MHD process would use fossil fuel, and produce fifty percent more electrical power per kilogram of coal, oil or gas than the fossil-fueled (or nuclear) power plants we are still using today.

The power companies loudly proclaimed that this was one research program that good ol' private enterprise was going to handle by itself. Uncle Sam wasn't going to get his sticky fingers on this baby, as he did in the nuclear business.

By the middle 1960's, the MHD process had been tested well enough so that Avco was ready to build a pilot power plant. Cost, about thirty million dollars. Suddenly Uncle Sam was the power companies' favorite relative. They declined to risk that much of their own money, and tried to get the Federal Government to make the investment.

The Federal Government was preoccupied with Vietnam and other problems, and didn't care about MHD or energy problems. The pilot plant got built, all right. And it's operating right now. In Moscow.

It wasn't until 1970 that Avco was able to put together a combination of Federal and industrial support to get moving again on MHD. During those five wasted years, a good deal of the oomph went out of the MHD research effort. Technical teams don't mothball easily. People left the program and got interested in other areas. The MHD effort is now at just about the place it would have been in, say, 1965—thanks to the foresight of the electric utilities' managements and the US Department of the Interior's experts.

That kind of thinking—or actually, lack of thinking—is the real reason for the energy crisis. There is no shortage of resources. There is no lack of technological skill. There has been a lack of interest both in industry and government in doing anything to head off the problem. Of course, now that the dam has burst, the barn's burned down, and the wolf's inside the door, everyone is following the classic response pattern of panic:

"When in trouble or in doubt, run in circles, scream and shout."

What needs to be done seems both clear and relatively straightforward. We must:

1. Develop new sources of energy that don't require fossil fuels. From steam power to thermonuclear fusion, we should be pushing on *all* practical ideas.

2. Utilize nuclear energy much more fully. Most of the hold-up in fission power has been due to the public's concern about radiation hazards and thermal pollution of water. Both these problems are solvable by proper application of known technology, *and an absolutely honest policy of public relations.* The people will support fission power plants once they are convinced that they are safe and won't destroy the local water resources.

3. Our own deposits of fossil fuels should be utilized, with as little harm to the environment as possible. Strip mining can devastate a landscape, true enough. But it may be possible either to get the coal in other ways or to reclaim the landscape after the mining operations have moved on. Moreover, it's technologically possible to convert high-sulfur coal into a cleaner fuel, such as natural gas. These environmental protection steps will be expensive, but they could be funded jointly out of the oil companies' excessive profits and public taxes.

4. Most importantly, we must obtain the leadership and sense of direction that is so conspicuously lacking at the moment. The Space Race was won the moment that John F. Kennedy decided to focus our efforts on putting a man on the Moon. Regardless of why he came to that conclusion, once he established the goal, we quickly outstripped the Russians and turned a once-scary situation into a no-contest.

It's grimly ironic that the scientists and engineers, who have been abused both by the radical left and the conservative right, who have had their funding slashed and their laboratories closed, who have been pilloried for being tools of the Pentagon and impractical eggheads—the scientists and engineers are the ones who will actually pull us out of the energy crisis.

It may take ten years, although the results of a really strong, vital program will begin to be felt much sooner than that. The White House is currently planning to spend ten billion dollars over the next five years on energy research and development. Dollar numbers in the Nixon Administration don't always mean a lot, because many games are played with such figures. But it seems clear that what's needed is more like a hundred billion dollars over the next ten years.

That would be an annual rate of funding about twice the size of the space program in its heyday. Considering the effects of inflation and the seriousness of the problem, that figure isn't extravagant.

We have the resources, the talent, the technology to solve the energy crisis. The question is, do we have the guts, the heart, the leadership, the will to get the job done?

Returning to Patrick Henry, he answered his own question in the same speech: "Sir, we are not weak, if we make a proper use of the means which the God of nature has placed in our power. . . . The battle, sir, is not to the strong along; it is to the vigilant, the active, the brave."

Can you *imagine* what fiery Patrick would be doing in Washington today?

Teaching Science Fiction

This one is really self-explanatory. The leggy blonde really did teach a science fiction course, on the qualifications mentioned in the Editorial. I really was the science consultant on *The Starlost*, a traumatic experience that led to my writing a novel called *The Starcrossed* (published by Chilton in 1975 and in paperback by Pyramid in 1976).

Science fiction courses are being taught at several hundred colleges and universities in the US this year. No one has been able to make an accurate count of how many high schools and junior highs are also giving short courses in science fiction.

Science fiction is also becoming a very popular item in the golden hills of Hollywood. There are literally dozens of feature-length movies and new TV serials being made on science fiction themes and subjects.

This could be very wonderful. It could also be very disastrous.

Those of you with stomachs strong enough to watch a few episodes of the TV series *The Starlost,* may have noticed that my name was among the list of credits at the finish of the show. I was listed as "Science Consultant." This is something like being Science Adviser to the Nixon Administration: you can give advice, but don't expect it to be taken.

In effect, my association with *The Starlost* has been an experience in teaching science fiction. An experience that ended in total failure and disillusionment. More on that in a moment.

It seems to me that teaching science fiction is not the easiest thing in the world to do. Yet, in most of the colleges and universities that offer science fiction courses, the qualifications of the teachers— *in the field of science fiction*—are either vanishingly small or totally nonexistent.

This is where a possible disaster lurks for those of us who love this field.

We expect, with some justification, that a burgeoning of interest in science fiction on campuses and in movies and TV, will bring about a sizable increase in the numbers of people who can enjoy science fiction. For purely esthetic reasons, this is highly to be desired. Science fiction has been a ghetto literature for far too long; it's time that we took our rightful place in the limelight of American fiction. The greater the number of readers and viewers who enjoy and appreciate science fiction, the stronger and healthier our field will be. We will get more, better, and more varied writing talent devoted to science fiction. And, strictly on the mercenary side, the bigger our family of readers and viewers, the more prestigious and financially rewarding will the field become.

But if this interest on campuses and in the entertainment world is bungled, if it turns people away from science fiction instead of toward it, then we've lost a magnificent opportunity and doomed ourselves to another generation of literary and artistic ghettoization.

I have seen, at first hand, some of the problems of teaching science fiction, both on campus and in the hectic atmosphere of a television series. Let me tell you about the TV business first.

The Starlost was Harlan Ellison's creation. With typical *élan* and imagination, Harlan envisioned a TV series set on a thousand-mile-long starship that was carrying hundreds of separate national, cultural and social groups to colonization among the stars. The ship was damaged and for centuries it has been drifting, while its various groups of colonists remained locked in their separated environmental domes, each of them fifty miles in diameter. They lost all memory of the ship and its original purpose over the course of many generations.

Not the world's most original science fiction plot, but one that has been the backbone for many good stories. Harlan's idea was to turn this series into a "novel on television," and have each episode advance the total plot of the story, so that over a three-year course the entire story is developed and brought to a dramatic conclusion.

Good thinking. But it overlooked some of the facts of the television industry.

Among those bitter facts was one central obstacle: the show was not bought by a network for prime time broadcast. Rather, it was sold in syndication. Every major city in the US bought the show—a sign of their interest. But, since the networks control the prime evening hours of eight to eleven, the individual stations could not broadcast *The Starlost* during prime time. In most cities, it was being shown at seven PM, either on Friday or Saturday.

This simple fact—lack of a prime time slot—turned *The Starlost* from a bold venture into a travesty of its original concept. For the producers of the show decided that they would not put into it the money that was required to make it live up to its original promise. They had already contracted for Keir Dullea to play the leading male role in the series. That was the last big-money decision they made.

It was all nickels and dimes from there on in.

I agreed to work with Harlan and the people who were actually doing the show, as a science adviser. If you want to see excitement, pathos, burning passions, adventure, intrigue and all the other goodies of the drama . . . then you should have watched what was going on behind the cameras when the show was being put together. What got into the scripts was bland. And what got onto the videotape was rancid.

As far as my science advice was concerned, the production crew listened very politely and thanked me profusely, then went off and did it their own way. I read scripts that were absolutely ludicrous, scientifically. I pointed out the problems with each script, in great detail, and suggested solutions to the problems, or alternatives to the story situations that led to the problems.

I could have just as well tried climbing Mt. Everest on my hands, for all the good it did.

After watching one show in its entirety, as it was aired in New

York, I quit *The Starlost*. I asked that they take my name off all the shows that I worked on, but they didn't even manage to do that.

Why should this have come to pass? Everyone connected with the show was a fairly competent professional in his or her field, qualified to produce reasonably solid television drama.

But they were not qualified in the critical area of science fiction. Harlan got so disgusted that he quit the show long before I did, and wisely took his name off the list of credits. He substituted his Writers Guild registered pen-name, Cordwainer Bird, which is Harlan's way of giving the bird to those who displease him.

Without Harlan's driving force and SF knowledge the series foundered. No one connected with the show on a day-to-day basis had the slightest understanding of science fiction. And, from the results, it's obvious that a strong understanding of our field's special attitudes, background and capabilities is a prime requisite for any successful show.

My own comments on the scientific side of the scripts would not have been enough to give the show a consistently good science-fictional look, even if my comments had been heeded.

Thus, people who are adequate writers, editors, directors, actors, special effects experts, et cetera—but who lack the special insights of science fiction—have produced a science fiction series that was dreadful.

While hardened science fiction fans may have watched *The Starlost* simply because it *was* science fiction, and because there was occasionally something interesting going on, it's impossible for me to believe that this show attracted any new fans to science fiction. An uncommitted TV watcher would see one episode and tell himself, "If *that's* science fiction, I'm going back to *I Love Lucy*."

Is the same thing happening on campus?

Those of us who love science fiction think it's wonderful that all those schools are giving courses in SF. But I recently had the somewhat shaky experience of meeting a lovely, leggy, blonde engineer who was, in her spare time, teaching a science fiction course at an eastern technical college. It was a shaky experience because, when I asked her how she was chosen to teach the course, she told me this story:

"I went to the dean and told him we ought to have a science fiction course. He agreed. Then he asked me who would teach it. I said I would. He asked me what my qualifications were. I said I'd read *The Martian Chronicles* and *Stranger in a Strange Land* and all that. He said, 'Well, that makes you the local expert. OK, you can teach the course.' "

I can imagine myself going up to the head of the anthropology department at a similar school and telling him that I'd like to teach an anthropology course. When he asked for my qualifications, I'd say, "Well, I've read Carleton Coon and Margaret Mead and all that stuff."

The point is, there is a certain body of knowledge that should be required of anyone who teaches a course in science fiction. Our field is as complex as they come, with its roots in literature, history, science and technology, social change, et cetera. No English department would let someone teach an English course unless he or she had some demonstrable qualifications in the field—papers published in the professional scholarly journals, or works of fiction published in the press. Something. Not just an earnest desire.

There is a professional society devoted to teaching science fiction, called the Science Fiction Research Association. But it is doing nothing about setting and demanding professional qualifications among SF teachers. SFRA is so new, its leaders claim, that its main interest lies in getting dues-paying members so that the organization can become strong. It will accept membership from just about anyone: teachers, writers, librarians, even people who merely "express a sincere interest in science fiction."

This is not professionalism, and it will not lead to a professional attitude toward the teaching of science fiction.

I am *not* advocating a stuffy, academic closed-mindedness toward who should be allowed to teach science fiction. That long-legged blonde might be a *terrific* teacher. But I don't think she—or many, many others like her—knows much about the history of our field, the influences of various writers, the interplay between technology and story subjects, and many of the other facets that are important for an understanding of SF.

The people who will get hurt first by this are the students. Those who take a science fiction course because they're seriously interested in the field will get short-changed. Those who take an SF course because they're curious about science fiction will quickly get turned off by inadequate teaching. (There are also those who take SF courses because they're good for an easy credit; who ever flunked science fiction?)

In the longer run, all of us will be hurt, too. Because our field will not grow as it might if the majority of those students came away from their courses satisfied and eager to learn more.

It's happened to science fiction before. There was a boom in our field just after the end of World War Two, when the advent of nuclear weaponry made it clear to many who had scoffed at SF that we were speaking prophetically. That boom ended rather quickly. There was another flurry of interest just after Sputnik, in the late 1950's, but it petered out fast, too.

All through the 1960's, though, the interest in science fiction on campus had been steadily growing. And now it has become "respectable" enough to be considered legitimate material for classes.

Fine. But if these classes result in disillusionment, then these hard-won gains will evaporate, and it will take another generation before anyone can mention science fiction in "respectable" company again.

We have come a long way in *this* generation. There are many good teachers of science fiction. The basic idea of the Science Fiction Research Association is a good one, even though the chalkdust aura of academia seems incongruous in the science fiction area. There are even good movies and television shows being done, with solid science fiction ideas and stories. And more to come.

But I fear a variation of Gresham's law, in which the bad

teaching and *schlock* movies and TV shows will drive out the good ones.

This is something that SFRA and SFWA—Science Fiction Writers of America, the professional organization of the writers—should struggle against with every ounce of their strength.

There must be minimum standards for anyone who teaches a science fiction course. No less than there are standards for those who teach gym, history, criminology or English literature. SFRA could set out a suggested standard of qualifications, and urge colleges and universities to adhere to it.

There must also be minimum standards for the science fiction movies and TV shows that are being produced. But here, the standards will be made and enforced by the buying public, just as they have done for decades with magazines and books.

But wouldn't it be wise for SFWA to try to suggest to the Hollywood moguls that a science fiction show should have competent science fiction advice, just as a medical show has at least a pharmacist hanging around?

And it would be even wiser if the advice were heeded.

Teaching Science Fiction Revisited

When Jim Gunn read "Teaching Science Fiction," he responded with this piece, which we ran as one of our infrequent Guest Editorials. (I love Guest Editorials; they save me the trouble of being brilliant for a month.) Jim, of course, is not only one of the best science fiction writers working these days, he is also a Professor of English at the University of Kansas. Here he presents the academic point of view about science fiction teaching.

The science fiction ghetto may be breaking up, but signs of the ghetto mentality still lurk among us: those who have possessed science fiction for so long that they consider her their own look upon any glance at a larger audience as proof of infidelity. A basic distrust of strangers, particularly those who use a different language, and a possessiveness about ghetto culture breed fear of those who would integrate ghetto dwellers and their arts into the general culture, and nourish an inner conviction that separatism might be best after all.

Our insecurity, our feelings of inferiority, make us suspicious of overtures from outside. Our history and our natures render us incapable of enjoying booms without dreading busts. We are, let us face it, a bit paranoid.

Professor Philip Klass (who teaches science fiction at Pennsylvania State University and writes it—alas, too infrequently these days—under the name of William Tenn) has compared science fiction with jazz, and I have a vision of science fiction as a prescient jazz musician playing piano in a turn-of-the-century New Orleans cat house. As his fingers rock over the keys, he is saying to himself: "Look at that s.o.b. sitting over there in the corner taking notes. Pretty soon he's gonna start a band in Kansas City or Chicago and make real money while I'm still sitting here collecting nickels and dimes, and then some dudes what never saw New Orleans are gonna make fortunes writing this stuff—writing! you don't write jazz, you just play it—and guys in white shirts and black ties are gonna perform it in those big, fancy New York halls, and kids are gonna study it in schools—and hell! that ain't gonna be jazz!"

Maybe not, and maybe it ain't gonna be science fiction, but events march on as surely as the tides roll in, and nothing we do is going to change that fact. We might, of course, be able to control the nature of those events or the path of the tides.

The ghetto "us-against-them" attitude, which gave science fiction fandom its strength and science fiction writers their feelings of brotherhood, erupts today in concern about the teaching of science fiction, such as the Editorial in the June 1974 issue of *Analog.*

First let me throw away the first half of the Editorial. I don't wish to defend science fiction in movies or on television, which I have personal reasons to think is terrible. One may count on the fingers of three hands the movies which are both good movies and good science fiction. Motion pictures and television are committee efforts controlled by money, which is always conservative, and by people who know nothing about science fiction and care less. The wonder is not that there is not more art in the visual media but that there is any at all.

At the same time we should admit that science fiction publishers have been almost as guilty. The movies and television have turned off potential readers of SF—but so has SF. The monster movies of the Fifties turned people away saying, "If that is SF I don't want any more," but so did the BEM covers of the Thirties, Forties and Fifties. The only meaningful part of science fiction is the story and if the reader can fight his way through all the obstacles to reach it, he either will like it or he won't.

Second, I don't want to defend science fiction teaching, since no one has sufficient information about it to either praise or condemn. Nor is this a defense of academic criticism, to which Sturgeon's Law applies fully as much as to science fiction. What I hope to do is bring a little perspective to the discussion of science fiction teaching, and what I wish to discuss are two issues raised by the June Editorial: the qualifications of science fiction teachers and

48

the effect of the teaching of science fiction upon potential new readers.

I'll grant immediately the Editorial's assumption that most science fiction teachers do not know enough about science fiction—not as much, certainly, as you and I, nor perhaps as much as your average reader. Let me grant also that they are not going to teach their science fiction courses the way we would teach them; probably we will not agree with their approaches, their tastes, their conclusions, and their results. But this would be true of any courses that you and I might teach. I know that Harlan Ellison, who is a vocal critic of science fiction teaching, would not like my historical approach to the field, and I suspect that I would not approve of all his judgments about what is important.

Joanna Russ, Phil Klass, Jack Williamson, and I—science fiction writers and English teachers all—have different ideas about what a course in science fiction ought to be. Who is right, and who is to say which of us is right, or if any of us are right, or if we are not all right?

Every new discipline goes through a period of experimentation and discovery. Every new discipline begins with no qualified teachers. African Studies was a product of the Sixties: no qualified teachers. Popular culture courses are no older than ten or fifteen years, and American Studies is not much older. Anthropology split away from sociology after World War Two in many universities, and departments of journalism, which originated in the early part of this century, became schools about the same time.

Schools of Business date back to the Twenties, most of them, and began with no qualified teachers. Schools of Education came about the turn of the century ... We can simplify the whole historical discussion by pointing out that departments originated when Eliot (of the famous five-foot shelf) introduced the elective system into Harvard when he became president in 1869. At that time, incidentally, the high school was virtually nonexistent (500) and compulsory primary education was just beginning to gain momentum across the nation.

And there were no qualified teachers.

So—science fiction teaching is going to go through the same process of accumulating experience and exchanging ideas and improving itself, and will never reach a stage where either the qualifications of the teachers or their agreement about subject matter will equal those in the sciences. The humanities have no objective measurements, no duplicatable experiments; they aim at increasing sensitivity, improving the ability to read with understanding, and providing the breadth and depth of intellectual experience which will encourage the making of wise choices.

They don't always succeed.

In the humanities, each teacher chooses his own texts and his own approach to the subject; each does what he can, in the best way he can. Professional organizations do not exist to determine qualifications—such determinations are made at the college or departmental level by the teacher's peers and sometimes his students—but to provide means of communicating among teachers and scholars in the field. In the early stages of the development of a discipline, professional organizations collect and observe and provide a central point for people to gather and discuss what they are doing, much as Milford in the Fifties and SFWA in the Sixties did for science fiction writers.

Moreover, teachers of science fiction are not just in English but in history, sociology, engineering, political science, anthropology, religion, philosophy, chemistry, physics, and many more disciplines, no doubt.

Science fiction teaching will develop its own criteria, its own canon, its own tools, and we can agree on this—it behooves those of us who have vested interests in its welfare to contribute our ideas and see that they are heard. Many of us, therefore, are active in the Science Fiction Research Association, attend scholarly meetings, lecture there and at other colleges, prepare histories and texts, write articles, and provide other materials useful in teaching, such as the lecture films about science fiction, featuring science fiction writers and editors, that we have been producing at the University of Kansas.

Many experienced writers and editors in the field have been supplying teaching materials and guidance. Robert Silverberg's *The Mirror of Infinity*, with critical essays by science fiction writers, has sold well, as has Harry Harrison's *The Light Fantastic* and his high school anthology (with Carol Pugner) *A Science Fiction Reader.* Jack Williamson has written his study of the early work of H.G. Wells, Brian Aldiss, his *Billion Year Spree,* Donald Wollheim, his *The Universe Makers.* Reginald Bretnor brought together the contributions of fifteen science fiction writers in his *Science Fiction, Today and Tomorrow*; and Frank Herbert has his name on an anthology for the academic market (along with three collaborators), entitled *Tomorrow, and Tomorrow, and Tomorrow* . . . Harlan Ellison has announced that he is collaborating on another science fiction text. My history of science fiction, *Alternate Worlds,* will be out in the spring of 1975.

True, other texts unsanctified by the name and ideas of a science fiction writer are proliferating. Many of them do not share our viewpoints—even those we have in common—and some of them clearly are using science fiction for their own ends. But who among us is not?

There is even a "Cliff's Notes" on science fiction, which some automatically would call the ultimate rape of science fiction by the academic world, but, as a matter of fact, the author, an L. David Allen at the University of Nebraska, put together a useful book with some illuminating concepts and some insightful analyses.

Many SF authors and editors have bemoaned the effect of academic criticism on science fiction. The dead hand of academic criticism will kill science fiction just as it killed poetry and the mainstream novel, they say. I think we can dispose of this bugbear easily. If science fiction has any vitality, criticism won't kill it. For one thing, few people read academic criticism—certainly not the readers of science fiction—and so long as writers do not accept the critics as final arbiters, they might even learn something about why they do what they do and why it works.

Science fiction traditionally has been concerned with the what, seldom the why. We have known, as readers and writers, that science fiction was different, but our explanations of the reactions have been unsatisfying. Periodically critics have sprung up among us and done us good by providing unifying theories, but their work has been limited and sporadic and seldom linked to the complete body of literature, of criticism, and of psychological experience. For a long time science fiction writers have needed literary feedback, criticism from sophisticated critics; now we well may get it. Not that we'll like it, not that much of it will not be dull and some of it unintelligent or even unintelligible, but we should not reject it outright—there are wise and intelligent literary judges outside our ranks and we can profit from their judgments. But we should not take it, nor ourselves, too seriously.

Finally, the feeling among SF people that the boom comes just before the bust: we have seen it happen before and our apprehensions overwhelm us when we see a boom approaching. There must be something wrong with it, and there must be something wrong with all those classes in science fiction being taught in colleges and universities, in high schools, and junior high schools, and even in primary schools. The kids will be turned off.

Let us grant that good teaching, enthusiastic teaching, will turn on more students to science fiction than bad teaching, incompetent teaching, dull teaching. But this is true of any subject, and the level of teaching is never as high as it ought to be. A good teacher can make learning the times table exciting, and a bad teacher can turn science fiction into pedantry.

But is this true? Most of what is read in high schools is cherished for its historic importance; much of it is valuable, much of it is difficult, and much of it is dull. A good teacher can make it meaningful, can demonstrate its relevance, can even make it exciting, but he must be *good*.

In this desert of irrelevance, a science fiction story cannot help but stand out like a refreshing oasis of story and significance; a bad teacher must work hard to make it dull. Generally the teachers of SF courses are not the bad teachers. The ones who volunteer to teach such courses may not be as knowledgeable as we would like them but they are, I suspect, enthusiastic, open, and experimental. A bad teacher would rather teach what he has always taught.

One more encouraging aspect—science fiction usually is an elective, fulfilling no requirements. Science fiction courses have achieved their popularity in high schools as part of senior (now junior or even sophomore) English electives: students ask for such courses. They are not being required to read Asimov and Bradbury in the way they are required to read Shakespeare and Dickens. Some students choose science fiction as the least of evils, perhaps, but it may be assumed of them that they never would have come to science fiction at all if it were not offered at their school; some of them, inevitably, will get turned on.

Let us look at the numbers involved. Science fiction, Phil Klass has said, is the mass literature of the very few. Traditionally science fiction has attracted several hundred thousand regular readers and perhaps an equal number of casual readers; these figures have not changed much since Hugo Gernsback founded *Amazing Stories* in 1926, I suspect. At least the circulations of the leading SF magazines have remained relatively constant: *Amazing* printed about 150,000 copies in its early years, *Analog* now, about 180,000. Most of the booms we have come to dread have been in publishing, not in readership. Until now.

The number of paperback titles published and bought—though in smaller print runs than in the Fifties—is evidence of a substantial increase in the casual readership of SF, primarily among young people; and if we do not include in our understanding of "regular" the reading of magazines, perhaps of regular readers as well. They are a paperback generation; they do not, I am sorry to say, read magazines. Out of 150 students surveyed in my class a couple of years ago, only 12 bought as many as one magazine a month, compared with 74 who bought at least one paperback each month.

The reasons for this are speculative and need not concern us here. Perhaps all readers should come to science fiction as we came to it—as a glad and personal discovery. But let me point out that in my class of 150 students, only 39 had what they defined as considerable experience with science fiction compared with 51 who had some, 52 who had slight, and 6 who had none.

Across the nation 500 college and university courses may deal with science fiction in one way or another; if the classes average 30 students each, some 15,000 students are being exposed to science fiction. Of these, probably 10,000 were not regular readers of science fiction before entering their classes.

In high schools, readership experience with science fiction must be even less. If there are 500 college courses, there must be 3,000 high school courses averaging 30 students each (both figures are conservative); and that means 90,000 students exposed to science fiction every year, of whom perhaps 70,000 are coming to science fiction for the first time. A minimum of 80,000 new readers are being recruited. At this rate the readership of science fiction stands to grow rapidly in the years ahead.

If—I can hear the skeptics say—the students are not turned off. Aside from my conviction that students exposed to science fiction in the classroom will find it so attractive, so fascinating, that they will be turned on rather than off, I can offer two experiences in support of the notion that they are not being turned off. I did a follow-up study on my class two years ago—the returns were smaller; it was optional and the end of the semester—because I too was curious about the effect of the class on readership. Two students reported that their interest in science fiction had been decreased, 25 that it had been increased, and 11 that it had not affected their interest (perhaps because it already was as high as it could go). Twenty said they expected to read more science fiction, 2, less, and 19, about the same.

The second experience was more recent. In a trip to Auburn University, I was asked to visit a class in which science fiction was being used by an assistant instructor (a graduate student) to teach freshman composition. Aha! I thought. Here is the classic test. If science fiction could survive this, it could survive anything.

I asked the students what they thought of the readings. One of them, an attractive freshman named Leah, said, "I didn't understand some of it." (It turned out that what she mostly didn't understand was an excerpt from Loren Eiseley's *The Unexpected Universe* and perhaps J.G. Ballard's "Terminal Beach.")

I asked what she thought about the course, and she said she didn't like to write a term paper about something she didn't understand.

"Ah," I said, "then will you be reading any more science fiction?"

"Oh, yes," she said. "I really enjoyed it."

It is the Leahs of the world, who never would have come to science fiction on their own, who have been exposed to it in high school or college, who find it enjoyable, who restore our faith in science fiction to overcome the handicaps of garish covers, miserable movies, terrible television, and even the teaching of science fiction.

The story's the thing. Sure, let us work to improve the teaching of science fiction. But only the stories can turn people on, and only the stories can turn them off. If the standards of science fiction remain high, if they continue to be raised even higher, if the writers, at least in part, broaden the appeal of their work so that it can be read and enjoyed by Leah and her friends, then we need not worry about the growing future audience for science fiction.

Teaching the Teachers

The first time Jim Gunn and I met after his Guest Editorial appeared in the magazine, we cooked up the idea of a summer Institute to teach science fiction to the teachers who wanted to teach science fiction courses. Jim got the University of Kansas to sponsor the first Institute, and this Editorial was a report on my few days there. It's disheartening, but enlightening, that the second Institute, scheduled for the summer of 1976, had to be cancelled because of lack of interest among the teachers. Apparently, the teachers want to teach SF, but not necessarily learn about it.

Everything's up to date in Lawrence, Kansas.

Amidst the pleasant green hills of the University of Kansas' Lawrence campus, they're teaching science fiction to the teachers of science fiction courses. And at the University's Space Technology Center, they could (if asked) teach NASA's public relations people a few things about the real benefits of the space program.

Science fiction first.

As regular *Analog* readers know, our June 1974 issue featured an Editorial which took to task those poorly qualified (and, in many cases, totally unqualified) teachers who give science fiction courses at the university and secondary school levels. A stream of letters from unhappy students poured into the *Analog* office after that Editorial, most of them from students bemoaning the fact that the teachers knew less about SF than the students themselves. Many of the letters came from students who were angry because their teachers openly loathed science fiction and were determined to brainwash the classes into hating it. A few letters came from irate teachers who insisted they were doing the best job they could.

James Gunn, one of the top science fiction writers and a professor of English at the University of Kansas—where he regularly gives a science fiction course—wrote an answering Guest Editorial for our November 1974 issue. He pointed out that science fiction is a "new boy" on campus, and that the teachers are gradually groping toward a satisfactory way of handling the subject.

The next time Jim and I met face to face (in Minneapolis, if memory serves) we braced each other with the idea of producing a course in science fiction *for the teachers.* I remembered back to the mid-Fifties, when I had been writing movie scripts for the Physical Sciences Study Committee—a group of the nation's leading physicists who, fed up with the poor quality of incoming physics freshmen, decided to build a new course in high school physics. They quickly learned that teaching modern physics to the students was easy, if the teacher knew the subject. So each summer the PSSC people set up special seminars to teach the teachers.

Jim had similar ideas, and suggested that the University of Kansas might sponsor a summer Institute on the teaching of science fiction. We further planned to get some of the top science fiction writers to come to the Institute for a few days each, to tell the teachers what the field is like from the inside. The money for this would come, we hoped, from donations from the science fiction publishers.

Those were the plans. The results were somewhat less than we had hoped for, though much better than we had feared.

The University of Kansas generously agreed to sponsor the three-week-long Institute. But by the time the necessary University approvals were granted and the arrangements made, it was almost the end of the academic year. Hurried notices were sent out to the academic community, and a tiny blurb was squeezed into the July issue of *Analog.* Most teachers make their summer plans early. This fact, combined with the sickly state of the economy, kept the attendance at the first Institute down to twelve teachers—almost all of them from the Kansas area.

The publishers failed to support the Institute almost entirely. Condé Nast Publications sponsored my appearance there. Only Prentice-Hall Publishing Corporation, through its Pren-Hall Foundation, contributed the funds for another author's appearance. No other publisher put up a penny. Several authors made their own way to Lawrence, including Gordon R. Dickson, John Brunner, Robert Bloch, and Harlan Ellison.

The local science fiction fans, hearing about all this, arranged a science fiction convention in nearby Kansas City for the weekend of July 18-20. Several of the authors attended, and the Institute's teachers had their minds slightly blown by the sight of a few hundred science fiction fans cavorting. (Kansas City will be the site of the 1976 World SF Convention, by the way. Robert A. Heinlein will be the Guest of Honor.)

In all, the Institute was a success. Despite the small turnout, all those who attended—including the guest authors—learned a good deal about the problems of teaching science fiction and their potential answers. The University was pleased enough with the results to go ahead and sponsor a second Institute, which will run from June 6 through 25. (Applications must be received before April 15; write to James Gunn, English Department, University of Kansas, Lawrence, Kansas 66045.)

If I could find any fault with the Institute, it was that there was too much emphasis on the history of science fiction as a literary genre, and not enough stress on the various fields of human endeavor that *make* science fiction: such as scientific research, sociology, politics, history, technological developments, et cetera. In the coming Institute, perhaps the participants can examine the techniques of team-teaching SF, with contributions from each of these fields as well as from English literature.

Of course, I was particularly interested in how *Analog* can be used to help teach science fiction. In previous meetings with SF teachers, particularly those associated with the Science Fiction Research Association, I had gotten the impression that those who teach "the literature of the future" insist on doing so out of thirty-year-old books. The teachers prefer the old standbys because they know what's in them, and a body of critical appraisal tells them what they should say to their classes about the books. *Analog*, being new and different each month, would force the teachers to read, think and decide for themselves. A fate many teachers are reluctant to embrace.

The teachers at the Institute were enthusiastic about *Analog*, however. They suggested that they could use the magazine if they had enough copies of one issue to distribute to each student in the class. Then that one issue of the magazine could serve as one of the "texts" for the course.

Analog would be glad to cooperate in this kind of experiment. Any teacher who wants a package of one issue of the magazine should write directly to me, and we will try to get the right number of magazines to the classroom, at our special rate for educational institutions.

(Special note: James Gunn's handsome history of science fiction, *Alternate Worlds*, has just been published by Prentice-Hall. It is lavishly illustrated, and if you can't afford the $29.95 price, at least urge your local library to get a copy.)*

Meanwhile, across the road from the University's main campus is the beautiful, modern and efficiently designed headquarters of the Space Technology Center. Very quietly, without much fuss, the students and professional staff there are passing on the benefits of the space program to the farmers, ranchers, mayors and taxpayers of Kansas.

A century ago, cattle ranchers hired riders—the John Wayne kind of cowhand—to guard their herds, to inspect the open range and check on the encroachment of woodlands and scrub growth that cut down on the available area of grassland, to check on the quantity of water available, and its quality. Today, a single photograph from an Earth Resources Technology Satellite (ERTS) can give that kind of information for the entire state. And more.

Farmers need early warning of crop disease. Urban planners need to know how many new houses are actually being built in the suburbs. City councils need to know just where the pollution in their rivers comes from. Taxpayers need to know why they're being asked to spend billions each year on the space program.

* A paperback edition has since been published.

NASA's public relations experts have always centered their hoopla on the manned space programs, partly because they're the most expensive items on the budget and partly because it seemed easier to glamorize the astronauts than an inert chunk of metal and electronics.

But maybe NASA's super-salesmen should be glamorizing the men and women who work in places like the University of Kansas' Space Technology Institute. These are the highly-skilled (and often lowly-paid) people who take those satellite photos and readout tapes and translate them into *information* that lowers costs for farmers, ranchers, supermarket customers, and taxpayers.

Make no mistake about it. Manned spaceflight is vital, as almost every reader of this magazine must know. The money spent on manned spaceflights is largely an investment in future technological capabilities. The point is, the investments we've already made are now paying dividends. Relatively unheralded satellites such as ERTS are paying off *now.* NASA should be highlighting this, especially when there are no "glamor" manned flights in view for five years, and the tax bills for the Space Shuttle are becoming very vulnerable to shortsighted Congressional cutpurses.

The Shuttle is not merely NASA's hope for the future. It is our hope, too; every one of us. Once the Shuttle begins to operate, the cost of placing payloads in space will go down dramatically, and the benefits everyone receives from space hardware will go up—just as dramatically. It would be a wise strategy to show the American taxpayers what we are already getting from space. Not what's going to happen ten years from now, but what's happening today. NASA has a strong and effective answer to the taxpayer's impatient, "But what's in it for me?"

The main thrust of the space program development from now to the end of the century will have to be the goal of reducing the costs of placing payloads in orbit. We have the hardware, right now, to do anything from checking the level of the water table across Kansas to checking the atmospheric constitutents of the outer planets. The big problem, the big expense, is boosting the hardware into space. The Shuttle is the first step toward a better, cheaper, more flexible space transportation system.

But NASA will never get to build those next steps, or the Shuttle itself, if the taxpayers feel that space hardware doesn't benefit them directly. Since the hardware *does* benefit them, isn't it time NASA started telling everybody about it?

The Idea Factory

It's bad enough to see the same hackneyed ideas rearing their battered heads week after week from the slushpile—that pile of manuscripts sent in by newcomers who've never been published before. This Editorial was written in exasperation with some of our more experienced professional writers who sometimes get lazy enough to rework those worn-out ideas themselves. In particular, the assumption that a tightly-knit empire of the Roman or British type can be established over interstellar distances seems to me to be one of the weariest, and silliest, pieces of shortcircuited thinking in the field today. Whatever the sociopolitical structure that evolves after we achieve starflight, it won't be an empire, I'm willing to bet. (Of course, a *good* writer can make even an Editor suspend his disbelief!)

There are nearly forty-five years' worth of ghosts peering over my shoulder. The complete file of *Astounding/Analog* issues, starting with the January 1930 *Astounding Stories of Super Science*, sits on the bookshelves behind my desk.

Since that very first issue, *Astounding/Analog* has been a magazine of ideas, a meeting ground for new concepts and opinions, a place that both writers and readers turned to when they wanted to sharpen their wits. Certainly, once John W. Campbell hit his stride as Editor, the magazine became a veritable Idea Factory.

In fact, due largely to Campbell's all-pervasive influence, science fiction has generally become known as "the literature of ideas." In a more disparaging tone, critics have pointed out that many science-fiction stories have The Idea as their hero, rather than human characters. In truth, we have all seen plenty of stories that were little more than a clever idea, sketched out in barely fictional form.

Ideas are important. They are not the be-all and end-all of science fiction, but they are a necessary ingredient in any good science-fiction story. Yet many outsiders have asked science-fiction writers, "Now that we've gotten to the Moon, what's left for you to write about?" And at least one prominent writer in this field, who has stopped writing science fiction, has reportedly said that all the good ideas have been used up, and there's nothing left to do but rehash them.

It would be simple to use Isaac Asimov's put-down. When

asked what's left to write about, the Good Doctor invariably says, "What's left? Only *everything!*"

But let's examine the problem a bit more deeply.

Every week, I see dozens of manuscripts that groan under the burden of the same tired old ideas, ideas that were rusted with age twenty and thirty years ago: the last two survivors of a global disaster turn out to be Adam and Eve; the "astronaut" struggling to get out of his "capsule" turns out to be a baby being born; the interstellar explorers find a new planet peopled by strange, barbaric, semi-intelligent creatures—the planet is Earth and the creatures are us. Most times these stories are written in the "tomato surprise" format: that is, the author saves the stunning surprise until the very last line of the story. It wasn't even a good technique when Verdi used it in *Il Trovatore.*

Then there are the stories that are instant clichés. Stories about the energy crisis or Watergate or campus unrest that would have made good science fiction ten years ago, but are not science fiction today, even though they may be set on Mars or Alpha Centauri. Science fiction is not "with it"; science fiction is—and has to be—*ahead* of it.

Most of these stories come from new writers who haven't yet learned how to dig deeply into their imaginations and come up with new ideas, original concepts. Still others get started on a good story line, but don't have the skill or courage to follow where the story logically leads. They frequently chicken out of a difficult plot situation by letting the protagonist die or commit suicide. Which is hardly the way to treat an audience of problem-solvers!

Yet there is a steady flow—albeit a slim one—of stunningly good stories by brand-new writers that are original, innovative, thought-provoking. In the twelve most recent issues of *Analog,* the Analytical Laboratory voting has given first place to two new writers and second place to eight; a remarkable showing when you consider that most of these issues featured serials and lead novelettes by "old pros" such as Gordon R. Dickson, Poul Anderson, Stanley Schmidt, Jerry Pournelle, and William Cochrane.

New writers can and do turn out good stories; stories that are rich in idea content *and* the special excitement of powerful fiction. And the readers respond to them accordingly.

The greatest disappointment of this Editorship is that some of the older writers, whose names and works we grew up on, have gotten out of the habit of tinkering with new ideas. They plow the same overworked ground in story after story, repeating themselves rather than seeking new territory. These stories don't get into *Analog.*

These older writers aren't the only ones who cling to the past. Whenever a letter arrives at this desk with the opening, "I've been reading *Astounding* for more than twenty years ..."—it's a complaint that the magazine is now featuring stories "that John would never have bought." Of course! John bought stories in the Sixties that he would never have bought in the Forties. Times change, tastes change. There has been a steady evolution. The Editor, the writers, the readers, the *world* keeps on changing, evolving, moving with the inexorableness of time's arrow.

No Editor would publish stories that are twenty years old in style and subject matter—not if he wanted to keep his audience. The nostalgia trip may be fine for anthologies, but magazines are the cutting edge of the science-fiction field, the place where the newest ideas and newest writers are tested.

Some of our readers are upset about the increasing realism in *Analog*'s stories, especially as regards sex and language. It's interesting to realize that John Campbell was attacked back in the 1930's for shaking the field by insisting on realistic stories. In those days, realism meant stories that had solid scientific backgrounds and believable characters. Some readers couldn't stomach Campbell's "new realism." But very quickly he built up an audience that would no longer accept the pseudoscience and cardboard characters of the earlier type of science fiction.

The great majority of today's audience also want realism in their science-fiction stories. Good science and good characterizations are taken for granted. The audience has matured to the point where some inclusion of sex in a story no longer sends everyone into a hot sweat. After all, the entire nation's attitude toward sex has liberalized considerably over the past generation. We're almost back to the pre-Victorian attitude, but not yet as far as the Elizabethan.

The same goes for what has euphemistically been called "strong language." Today's readers don't mind seeing in print the words that they hear and speak themselves every day.

This is not to say that *Analog* will become a porno magazine filled with obscenities. I would not buy a story just because it has sex and street language in it. But neither will I reject a story outright for that reason. The guiding principle is realism. In most science-fiction stories, putting in a sex scene or obscene language is totally unnecessary and detracts from the story. But in some, the characters' sexual behavior is an important part of the story, or the gutter language a character uses is a vital part of the characterization.

We've heard strong opinions from the readers on both sides of this matter. But an analysis of the AnLab voting shows that sex and language problems don't really affect the outcome very much; powerful stories place highly, no matter how much or how little sex and foul language is in them. (Incidentally, it wouldn't hurt if more readers made their feelings known by voting in the monthly Analytical Laboratory poll. All you need to do is send in a postcard with the stories in the current issue listed in your own order of preference. The first-place winner gets an extra cent a word for his story, second-place winner gets a half-cent extra, and the Editor gets to know in some detail just what your tastes really are. So put *our* money where *your* mouth is!)

Let's get back to ideas.

We've all seen countless stories featuring an interstellar empire. Has anyone stopped to think of what an interstellar empire would *really* be like? Because the chances are that the only interstellar empires the human race will ever see will be in science-fiction magazines.

All political organizations have a natural limit to their size, placed on them by the speed of communications available to them.

In ancient Greece, the limit of political cohesion was set by the distance a man could reasonably walk in a day: city-states. Ancient Rome, with its solid engineering and good roads made an empire that girdled the Mediterranean basin. The Mongols of the thirteenth century invented the pony express relay system and built an empire that spanned Eurasia from the Sea of Japan to the Danube.

If the speed of light is a limit on communications, then there can be no interstellar empires. The distances between the stars are so vast that it would take generations to get information from one star system to another. Even if we get around the light-speed limit in some manner, it would appear that starflight would take so much energy—like the energy output of a star itself to propel a modest-sized ship—that interstellar flight would be fantastically expensive and thus very rare. Instead of an empire, there would most likely be a loose confederation of stellar systems, linked tenuously by the occasional visits of prohibitively expensive starships.

Yet we keep seeing stories that blithely assume an interstellar empire with a political structure not too far removed from the Roman and British models. When is a writer going to sit down and figure out how an interstellar community might actually behave? Poul Anderson has come the closest to doing this, but the subject is vast enough for many, many writers to examine all the different permutations.

There's another piece of artistic shortchanging that too many writers pull on themselves. That's the story where the hero never sweats. No matter what heinous trap the villains have dumped him into, no matter how many generators have blown out, no matter that his girl has run off with an android and the extraterrestrials are merrily blowing up every city on Earth, Our Hero smiles grimly and does exactly the right thing. And he wins without even mussing his hair. The problem here is that the writer knew from the beginning that everything was going to work out OK, and he let it show in his hero's behavior.

All the action, suspense, problems are merely plot devices. We all know that the good guy will solve all the problems, conquer the baddies and win the girl. Instead of a story, we have a superman myth that gets more boring each time it's retold.

There are more editorial crotchets that we could examine, but I hope you get the drift of my leanings from these few examples. So much for worn-out ideas. Where are the new ones?

In the minds of the writers and readers, mostly. But here are a few you can mull over.

Science fiction has had its share of pirate stories. John Campbell himself wrote about air pirates, although most SF stories have dealt with piracy in space. Air pirates—hijackers—have become a reality. But modern hijackers don't use the same *modus operandi* as Cap'n Kidd and his swarthies, nor do they operate for the same motives. The technology and the society have changed; so have the methods and motivations of the pirates. Assuming that there will be some form of piracy once interplanetary commerce becomes fairly commonplace, what will it be like? And why? What will be the pirates' motivations and methods?

Space piracy? Sure—especially if we have a Third Industrial Revolution and begin utilizing the raw materials of the other planets and asteroids, and ship them back to factories in orbit around the Earth. What kind of society will *that* be? Who will be rich and who will be poor? Which nations will grow stronger; which weaker? How will the oil-rich nations fare when thermonuclear fusion provides our energy and the asteroid belt provides our raw materials?

Staying right here on Earth, how about a society built on individual responsibility? For example, we now have a welfare system that takes tax money from earners whether they like it or not, and provides welfare payments for nonearners. Many taxpayers have complained that they would sooner pay for voluntary charity than have taxes taken from them against their will. Suppose we adopted a system where taxpayers are given individual welfare recipients as their personal wards, and get tax deductions for them? The welfare recipient would go *personally* to his or her "guardian" for support. There are a million different stories there, and at least one of them should be titled "My Brother's Keeper."

Astrology has turned to modern technology for help; astrological forecasting services use computers to work out their mumbo jumbo (as Robert Heinlein suggested in *Stranger in a Strange Land*). The self-aware computer is a stock character in SF nowadays. But suppose a self-aware computer began making astrological forecasts for itself? And acting on them?

The ideas are there. The subject matter is just as open and wide as Isaac Asimov claimed. There's starflight, time travel, immortality, genetic manipulation, biofeedback, behavior control, telepathy, interplanetary colonization, the development of a "second generation" technology that turns one industry's pollution products into another industry's raw material.

But the most important thing to write about is *people.* Think of the stories you remember best, and the chances are you remember a character, a person whose problems and struggles moved you emotionally.

To paraphrase Alan Jay Lerner's paraphrasing of George Bernard Shaw, "By and large we are a marvelous race." The human race, that is. And *that* is what good stories are really about: people. People who face problems and strive to surmount them, who sometimes win and often lose but always *strive.* They may look decidedly nonhuman, and they may be anywhere and anywhen in the universe. But all good fiction is concerned with people, and the rest—the exotic backgrounds and clever ideas—are merely attempts to place the human spirit in a crucible where we can test its worth.

That's the ultimate idea of the Idea Factory.

By Their Fruits

This one came from the heart (and also possibly a little bit from the spleen). What shocked me about Watergate was the calm way the people took the whole thing. Until the very end, when they just-as-calmly made it quite clear that the most powerful individual human being on the planet had to leave office. And he did, without a shot being fired. Too bad it couldn't have been arranged for 1976; it would have been an apt Bicentennial reminder of who and what we are.

The trouble is, I'm a time-traveler.

I've stood on the wooden bridge in Concord, where a scared and badly-organized band of farmers briefly faced up to the trained professionals of the British Army. I've looked out at the Massachusetts countryside from that bridge and realized what those farmers knew: this land is worth fighting for.

I grew up during World War Two, and heard about a young Air Corps officer named Colin P. Kelly who kept his crippled B-17 aloft long enough for his crewmen to bail out safely, then dove the plane into a Japanese warship, killing himself. And of Joe Schmidt, the Marine from Philadelphia, who stayed at his machinegun during an all-night Banzai attack on Guadalcanal, despite being permanently blinded by a grenade explosion in the first few minutes of the battle.

Nearly every day I walk past the spot in New York where a young schoolteacher named Nathan Hale was hanged as a spy by the British. And I think to myself of all the young men over the past two-hundred-some years who have given their lives to preserve, protect and defend this nation. All those anonymous hundreds of thousands, who never spoke as eloquently as Hale, nor died as dramatically as Colin Kelly, but who put their lives on the line because—at heart—they were convinced that this nation is something worth fighting for, worth dying for.

And then I observe today's scene. I see men who swore on Holy Bibles, before television audiences that spanned the globe, to preserve, protect and defend the Constitution of the United States of America. I read the transcripts of their tape-recorded words, and see the consequences of their actions, and I realize that either they had no intention of taking their oaths seriously or they haven't the faintest idea of what the Constitution and our nation are all about.

I see men who have sworn to faithfully uphold the laws of the United States deliberately breaking those laws, ordering the CIA to spy on American citizens—which is specifically prohibited by law—while making pious public pronouncements about law and order. And I wonder what Hale, and Kelly, and Schmidt, and all the rest of what used to be called our honored dead would have done if they could have known what they were helping to bring about.

The Founding Fathers knew that our form of government is an experiment. Large-scale democracy, even in the indirect form adapted by the framers of the Constitution had never been tried before. Two centuries down the time stream, the experiment still has not produced definitive results. It just may be that large-scale democracy can no longer work in a society where the decision-making power is so far removed from the people.

By their fruits you shall know them.

Law and order cannot flow from a government that considers the laws as irrelevant and subsidiary to its political goals, any more than peace and fellowship can flow from the philosophy espoused in *Mein Kampf*.

And a democratic form of government cannot exist among a people who take little or no interest in the workings of government. The most insidious, deadly poison stemming from *l'affaire Watergate* is the lassitude and air of resignation among the voters. Any American citizen who blandly claims, "What can you do? All politicians are like that," is asking for more and worse than Watergate.

By their fruits . . .

When the Nixon Administration first came to office, and Vice President Spiro Agnew began to attract national attention by attacking the press and the electronic news media, my ex-newspaper-man's ears tingled. "Why attack a press that's been generally so favorable?" I asked myself. "Unless there's something going on that they don't want the press to find out," was the second half of my thought. No, I assured myself, that's just a knee-jerk reaction from an ex-reporter. It wasn't until nearly five years later that it turned out that Agnew himself had plenty to hide, including accepting bribes in the very office of the Vice President.

Jefferson looks like a saint from this distance in history, but during his lifetime he was attacked by the press in terms that would shock a modern politician. Yet when he became President, he allowed the Alien and Sedition Laws—John Adams's method of jailing those who publicly disagreed with him—to expire. Not only that, but the Jefferson who wrote about the inalienable rights of man also said:

"... were it left to me to decide whether we should have a government without newspapers, or newspapers without a government, I should not hesitate a moment to prefer the latter."

The man had faith in the American people! Fellow time-travelers, he had faith in you and me.

Maybe Jefferson was an airy theorist who made lovely pronouncements that didn't work in the rough-and-tumble of real-world politics? How about James Madison's thoughts on the subject:

"A popular Government, without popular information, or the means of acquiring it, is but a Prologue to a Farce or a Tragedy; or, perhaps both. Knowledge will forever govern ignorance: And a people who mean to be their own Governors, must arm themselves with the power which knowledge gives."

How many people do you know who got sick and tired of hearing about Watergate? How many American voters shut their eyes and ears to the doings of their own Government? How many German citizens did the same when the Nazis were carting off their neighbors to the death camps?

Corruption is an ugly word, but a time-traveler who scans the past two centuries of American history and studies the present political and social climate of the United States cannot help but feel that we have a very corrupt situation on our hands. And this corruption exists at the heart of American politics, among the voters, the people who have the power to make changes but lack the foresight and the guts.

The average voter simply does not exercise his or her sovereign power. Trotting out to the polling booth on election day is too late. The real power struggle lies in the very early days of the political campaigns, when the local and national party structures pick the candidates that end up on the ballot.

And look at the campaigns themselves. The candidates have become nothing but plastic images, parroting public relations slogans and evading every possible issue. When's the last time you saw a candidate behave the way Harry Truman did in 1948, when he insisted on a strong Civil Rights plank in the Democratic Party's platform? Even when told that the Southern delegates would walk out and form a third party, Truman preferred to keep faith with his conscience rather than sell out to the Dixiecrats. Can you picture any recent candidate, from the two Presidential candidates of 1972 on down to your local mayor or councilman, facing an issue so straightforwardly?

The real genius of the 1972 Presidential campaign was the way in which the Nixon campaigners were able to cut the electorate into myriads of tiny, self-seeking pressure groups, and promise each one of them that the particular little goodie that they wanted would be given to them by the Nixon forces. Aid to Israel? Sure, it's good for the Jewish vote. Reform the welfare system? No, that would frighten the blue collar vote. More defense spending? Yes, it'll win votes wherever there's a military base or a defense factory.

Seen narrowly, this is good politics. After all, it produced a landslide of votes, didn't it? But politics is more than winning elections. After the election, the winner must govern. Hopefully, he and his associates will govern wisely and, in Lincoln's phrasing, "for the people."

Taking this broader view, a time-traveler is tempted to

speculate that by dividing the electorate into self-seeking power groups, the politicians lost sight of the needs of the *nation* as a whole. What's worse, their pandering to the narrow interests of the voters allowed the voters to lose sight of the fact that we're all in this big socio-political experiment together, and what's good for your pocketbook in the short term might have disastrous consequences on your whole family's life style in the long run.

The social unrest, the energy problems, the inflation and economic recession that are making a shambles of our economy, the collapse of our educational system, the cynicism and despair among the people—all these are the result of taking the narrow, self-seeking view and avoiding the painful but necessary attack on the vast social and economic problems that beset us.

Nixon is not the sole villain in this scenario. Long before he reached the White House, the national political stance had become, "Here's your slice of the pie; don't worry about anything else." Whatever shortcomings John Kennedy might have had, at least he told us that his job wasn't to make life easy for us; he challenged us to do our best, and we reached the Moon as a result.

Science fiction teaches us to be time-travelers. We learn to think in terms of centuries, not years. And if we look forward only a few decades, we can see that real disaster awaits us—unless we stop our piecemeal, stopgap politics, and begin to come up with tough, real answers to the tough, real problems that face us. The dike is leaking badly, we're running out of thumbs, and it looks like rain.

The answers will not be easy to come by. Nor will they be very popular. For the fact is that our society must change. To most people, change is fearsome; they are terrified that they'll have to give up something that they've now got. The rioting in Boston over school busing has nothing to do with education; the good neighbors of South Boston fear an influx of poor blacks into their homeland. What they fear, they resist.

We need political leaders who can lead, rather than follow the results of the latest public relations poll, and give press-agent's answers to predigested questions. We will not get such leadership unless we demand it, and hold it accountable once it is voted into office.

In the final analysis, we need something beyond patriotism. I don't think it was merely patriotism that motivated men like Nathan Hale or Colin Kelly or Joe Schmidt. Or Jefferson, either, for that matter.

Too often, patriotism boils down to, "My country, right or wrong," or its modern evocation, "America, love it or leave it." It is possible to love this nation of ours and still realize its shortcomings. It is *necessary* to change our society, because without change it will soon die.

What's the word, the symbol, we're seeking? Perhaps it is *idealism.* An overworked word, a word that's often looked upon askance. A corny word. Yet it was the ideal of a free and democratic people that gave those Massachusetts farmers the backbone to stand up against British regulars. It was the ideal of the inherent liberty and dignity of all human beings that guided Jefferson's pen, and ultimately produced the Bill of Rights.

Colin Kelly wasn't thinking of the need for expanding markets for the US steel industry when he nosed his plane into its final suicide dive. Perhaps he should have been, but if he was thinking clearly at all, it was probably something about the absolute need to protect, preserve and defend the form of society that we have built in America.

Without the ideals, there is no nation. Merely a milling crowd of self-seeking, clamoring individualists who are all trying to be first in line for a free handout. That way lies dictatorship or anarchy.

With idealism, patriotism can be something to be proud of. We have enormous energy and power. A time-traveler, looking backward, sees that we have created the wealthiest, best-fed, longest-lived society in the history of the world. We have achieved political dominance on a worldwide scale, and backed away from creating an empire, not merely once but twice. We have reached the Moon, and done it with such casual ease that the world was astonished by it.

We have the energy, the power, the skills and strengths needed to solve the problems we face. Do we have the will? That is always the central question. The brain and muscle are there, but what's happened to our hearts?

By their fruits you shall know them.

This is the real tragedy of the Nixon Presidency, and the Watergate conspiracy, and the whole tenor of our modern public relations era of politics:

It has taken the idealism out of politics. It has taken the heart out of a once-proud and mighty nation.

Kelvin Throop Strikes Back

Kelvin Throop is a fascinating and very useful fellow, in addition to being quite mysterious. He answers his mail the way a polite Editor, anxious to avoid upsetting his faithful readers, could never do. Every response Throop wrote was in answer to a real letter that was on my desk at the time.

As faithful readers of *Analog* know, Kelvin Throop was first heard from in a communication sent to us by R.A.J. Phillips, and published in our July 1964 issue. At that time, Throop was an official in the snow-bound bureaucracy of the Canadian Department of Northern Affairs. One day he answered all the mail in his IN basket as honestly as an innocent child would—an innocent child who had suffered through years of frustration from dealing with malicious and pernicious idiots in government, industry, and private life.

Throop answered his mail with candor, vigor, and a large helping of caustic prose. Then he disappeared. Apparently he jumped out a window and dashed off into the wilderness.

He surfaced again, briefly, and his antics were reported by E. Silverman in the January 1966 *Analog.* Apparently Throop was at that time an executive in a small engineering firm that did some Defense work in the US. Again, his patience reached the boiling point, he answered his incoming mail as clearly and incisively as he could—and vanished once more.

He has returned.

At least, he apparently sneaked into the Condé Nast Building and found the *Analog* office, in the dark of one late January night. The ever-alert building security forces must have frightened him away, because the next morning, some of the incoming mail left overnight had been answered, but none of the letters had been posted.

In the interests of coaxing him into the light of day, if not the limelight of deserved fame, we are publishing his hastily-penned replies to the Editor's incoming mail. The world needs more people like Kelvin Throop, who is not afraid to call a spade a spade (or even a goddamned shovel). Herewith, his answers to a typical day's incoming mail, as he found it in the *Analog* office.

Dear Coward:

Since you didn't have the guts to sign your obscene letter or give a return address, I am sending this response to the Postal Service's dead letter office. Knowing the way the PO works, they'll probably get this to you overnight.

Although it was difficult to make sense out of your misspelled, four-letter prose, it seems that you don't like blacks, women, Jews, Mexican-Americans, or anyone else who can't goose-step in time to your primeval paranoia. No wonder you read science fiction: you certainly don't belong on *this* planet!

Cordially,
K. Throop

Dear Ms. Radlib:

I just don't see how we can use a female as the leading character in *every* story. True, every hero has had a mother, but many heroes accomplish their lofty feats in spite of, rather than because of, the women in their lives. And while I suppose it's possible to say "humankind" instead of "mankind," I do think it's just a bit clumsy to use terms such as "hero-person," "scientist-person," and "villain-person." Also, Mars and Venus are their *names* lady! If you want that changed, take it up with the astronomy-persons. Finally, your suggested new pronoun that combines "she," "he," and "it" into one short word is inadvertently funny, scatological, and would give our readers the wrong impression.

Love and kisses,
Kelvin Throop

Dear High-Shooter:

Your letter was sent to this office for response by the president of the corporation, to whom you addressed your complaint.

I'm deeply sorry that you are upset by mentions of sex in some of the stories. This frequently happens to readers who have not gotten past their infantile neuroses, and it must be very painful and confusing for you.

You are certainly entitled to your opinions, but you should address your letters to the man you're angry with. The corporation's president doesn't really believe that the entire publishing industry will collapse if you drop your subscription. And going over the Editor's head merely delays response to your letter.

By the way, I'm sending copies of this letter to the president of your corporation, your pastor, and your nearest psychiatrist.

Merrily,
Kelvin Throop

Dear Theologian:

I seriously doubt, as Einstein did, that God is perverse. You may believe that He's got nothing better to do than strew this planet with fossils that were all created in 4004 BC, just to mislead paleontologists, but my own belief is that the evidence for human evolution is on very firm ground. The fact that evolution is "still called a theory," as you so quaintly put it, does not mean that scientists regard it as an unproven hypothesis.

Considering some of the human beings on this planet, I don't at all mind being related to apes.

Thoughtfully,
K. Throop

Dear Mr. Brilliant:

Your invention sounds marvelous. Not only will it solve the energy crisis, but it will apparently create more energy than it consumes.

I'm not surprised that the Energy Agency, the Patent Office, NASA, and the Department of Defense have all turned down your overtures. Obviously they're jealous. Send your proposal to the Saudi Arabian embassy in Washington, so that the Arabs can see that their days of high-living are doomed.

I doubt that the Editor will want to publish an article about your invention. He always checks with Professor Maxwell and his equations before buying a science article, and your invention will conflict with the Laws of Thermodynamics. He's short-sighted that way, just as all the rest of them are.

Back to the drawing board!

Regretfully,
Kelvin Throop

Memo to (indecipherable):

I'm sorry, but the office staff here at *Analog* is just too small to take on an additional person, even though your nephew is a great "sci-fi" fan and never misses a rerun of *Star Trek*. As you yourself pointed out, a business office is no place to teach a college undergraduate how to spell.

K. T.

Dear Mr. Faithful:

Yes, you're right. There was a poem in the January 1975 issue. I'm sorry that this has caused you to cancel your subscription, especially since you've been reading *Astounding* and *Analog* since 1934. Perhaps Campbell wouldn't have done things that way, but he was always rather fond of dragons, actually.

Breathlessly,
Kelvin Throop

Dear Dr. Pencilbeam:

I have pored over your letter for some time now. While I will not pretend to be able to follow the math (although I found a few simple errors in addition at one point), I don't think it's details such

as mathematics that will make or break your theory. Several thinkers
have pointed out that Einstein was dead wrong, and Relativity is a
Zionist plot to destroy the minds of Western man. However, every
test of Einstein's theories seems to confirm his ideas, often to many
decimal places. Instead of writing counter-theories, why not produce
an experiment that *shows* Einstein's wrong?

Curiously,
K. Throop

Dear Friend:

According to the cover letter atop your 250,000-word
manuscript, you are doing the Editor the enormous favor of letting
him see this novel before any other magazine editor gets it. I'm sure
they'll all enjoy reading it, eventually. While it's perfectly true that
Analog could serialize this work in only ten or twelve installments,
some of our readers might have nervous breakdowns waiting to
amass all the issues.

On the other hand, a long novel written from the point of view
of a micro-organism that lives in the hero's intestinal tract is—to say
the least—a novel idea. Too bad that this photocopy of the original
manuscript is very faint, and the paper is battleship gray. I doubt
that the Editor's ophthalmologist will allow him to read more than
two pages of the manuscript per day. At that rate, you can expect
his decision sometime next year. Or the following one.

Good Luck,
Kelvin T.

Dear Mr. Vermeer:

I'm sorry, but it's impossible for us to work with artists who
can't come into the office for face-to-face ~~fights~~ discussions with the
Editor, Art Director, and Circulation Manager. You paint beauti-
fully, as everyone in your family does, but until color picturephone
service is initiated between New York and The Hague, we'll have to
struggle along with the likes of Freas, Schoenherr, Gaughan, *et al.*

Visually,
K. Throop

Dear Writer:

I can assure you that the Editor did indeed read your manuscript the first time you sent it in.

He also read it the second and third times, just to see if you had changed anything except the cover letter.

The reason he sent it back with a form rejection slip rather than a personal letter is that there was nothing he could say about the story except that it is poorly written, abysmally typed, lacking in invention, drama, suspense, and interest, and generally left him feeling sick to his stomach.

Satisfied?

Kelvin Throop

P.S. The plot worked fine when Heinlein used it, but it doesn't work so well when the invading extraterrestrials tie strings to the humans' wrists and ankles and turn them into puppets *literally.*

Dear Mr. Smith:

I realize that the current Editor is a left-wing crypto-communist bleeding-heart tool of the ADA. But your suggestion that welfare mothers be shot and their children sold to the dogfood industry strikes me as a bit harsh. True, this would lower grain prices somewhat, and make filet mignon slightly more affordable. Bully for you. The real problem with the nation's economy, however, is not too many poor people; it's too few rich. Get the distinction?

Economically,

K. Throop

And that's what Throop wrote. He must have answered about a dozen other letters that were also on the Editor's desk, but which have since disappeared. If you should receive a missive from him, try to track down the Post Office from which it was mailed. A computer-based analysis of his peregrinations indicates that Throop is heading westward, possibly toward Hollywood. The thought of him popping up in the motion picture or TV industry is shattering. But it feels *right.*

The SF Game

John Campbell used to boast that he'd read more lousy science fiction than anyone in the history of the world. After all, he read every manuscript sent in to the magazine from the moment he took over the Editorship in 1937 to his untimely death in 1971. I can't speak for him, but to me reading the slushpile is exhausting, sometimes infuriating, and—once in a great while, when a good story from a new writer pops up—the biggest thrill in the game. In this Editorial I tried to point out some of the neglected facets that go into writing science fiction, and to stretch the readers' (and potential writers') minds a little. Too little, maybe. We still don't get very many stories based on the startling breakthroughs that are coming out of the biology labs.

Whenever I'm invited to speak before a group of people who are not science fiction readers, someone in the audience inevitably asks, "Why are science fiction writers so good at predicting the future?"

The answer, of course, is that SF writers are not terribly good at predicting the future. In fact, they're not even trying to. It just happens that they're better at such predictions than any other body of prognosticators, amateur or professional.

To begin with, science fiction stories do not predict THE future because there is no such thing. Unless you believe in a totally fixed and immutable timestream (in which case it doesn't matter what you do, everything's frozen in cement already), then the future *must be* a series of events that have not yet happened, and therefore can be altered, changed, diverted, moved, shaped by myriads of individual decisions. There is no one certain future; there are countless possible futures, with every moment bringing new opportunities to hand.

Science fiction writers explore those many possible futures. Each SF story is an exploration of a potential future. If human history can be thought of as a migration of billions of people across the vast landscape of time, then the science fiction writers are the scouts who range far ahead and bring back occasional reports on what the territory up ahead is like, so that the main body of the people can choose their course more intelligently, avoiding the badlands and picking out the sunny, well-watered meadows and cool, green hills.

90

In a typical year, thousands of such glimpses of possible futures will be published in science fiction magazines and books. Almost every one of these "predictions" of the future will be dead wrong. The futures depicted in those stories will never come to pass. Yet there are more accurate and usable forecasts of the future in SF than in any other body of literature—including the meticulously researched reports of the professional, scientific futurologists.

How can this be? Scientific forecasting has become a respectable, specialized business. It originated with the RAND-type think-tanks of World War Two and the Cold War, and has now grown to include technological and business forecasting groups in almost every major industry in the United States, as well as in many Government agencies, especially the military.

Yet, if you read back over the futurologists' reports of just a few years ago, you find that they are hopelessly inaccurate. Business forecasts are more often wrong than right, military intelligence forecasts are notoriously short-sighted, and even as prestigious a book as Herman Kahn's *The Year 2000* has a quaint air of absurdity about it, with its total lack of foresight into the energy and raw materials crises, and the growing instability of American politics.

Forecasts made by professional futurologists grow increasingly inaccurate with time. The "technical assessment" group of a major corporation may make a rather good forecast of the market growth potential for a given product for the coming fiscal year, for example. But its forecast for five years ahead will usually be very unreliable. And a ten-, twenty-, or fifty-year forecast is probably worthless.

Science fiction predictions are just the opposite. In general, a science fiction story dealing with events of next year will be badly unrealistic. But a story set fifty or a hundred years in the future has a much better chance of being accurate than a futurological forecast.

Why? Because the futurologists have to stick to the facts! They can only deal with what they *know* is possible. They cannot handle the "wild card" possibilities. In 1960, no valid futurological forecast could be made on the assumption that the President of the United States would be assassinated. In 1975, no believable futurological assessment of the energy problem can include the possibility that intelligent aliens from an advanced civilization will give us cheap, efficient, pollution-free fusion reactors next year. Or next decade. Or ever.

Yet it is these unpredictable "wild card" events that shape history, just as much as the steady, extrapolatable progress in technical, social, and economic developments.

There's an old joke that a futurologist's forecast of the pollution problems of New York City in 1875 would have predicted that, by the turn of the century, the city would be buried under horse manure. Such forecasts today concentrate with equally narrow vision on the pollution problems of automobiles. Science fiction writers, however, predict teleportation booths and wonder what to do with all the freeways that have been built everywhere.

To a large extent, science fiction predictions are based on contemporary science. There is very little in SF's marvelous cornucopia of inventions that has not appeared first in the scientific journals. But, again, while the professional scientists concentrate their efforts on proving that their theory is correct, or that their experiment works, the SF writers can take that part of it for granted, and concentrate their efforts on examining how this new discovery or invention affects human beings.

To the scientists and engineers laboring over NASA's Space Shuttle, the problems of building a reliable, reusable spacecraft are the most important and difficult problems in the world. Yet science fiction writers blithely assume that the Shuttle not only will work, but that it will be the first generation of a steadily-improving series of spacecraft that make colonization of the Moon and cislunar space possible, profitable, and attractive.

The professional scientists are constrained to sweat over the problems. The professional SF writers are free to examine the results of solving those problems.

The professional futurologists are constrained to deal only with those future developments that can be logically extrapolated from current events. The SF writers can, do, and must include the

92

"wild card," unpredictable, unlikely events in their descriptions of the future.

Science fiction is always based on verifiable scientific fact. (Good science fiction, that is.) But if SF stuck strictly to the agreed-upon "facts" of science, it would be as shortsighted and pedantic as the scientific establishment itself. Science fiction uses those facts as a starting point to explore any and every cranny of the universe. A science fiction writer is free to invent any new science he can imagine—so long as his inventions do not contradict what is accepted as scientific fact today.

Thus SF writers can break the speed of light in their stories, despite the apoplectic reaction of most physicists. But if and when those physicists can present incontrovertible evidence (not mathematical treatises) that nothing in the universe can *ever* move faster than light, science fiction writers will begin to live within that constraint.

Most biologists react with equal apoplexy to science fiction stories that deal with human cloning, or genetic engineering, or behavioral control such as Huxley described in *Brave New World.* The biologists fear that such SF stories present them as modern-dress Dr. Frankensteins who are tampering with the sacred materials of life itself.

Which, of course, is exactly what they are doing. They have a right to be upset about SF stories that show only the sensational, dangerous, anti-human possibilities of current-day biological research, just as the physicists have become justly sensitive about SF stories depicting mad scientists who want to rule the world by creating new devastating super-nuclear weapons.

As Joe Allred pointed out in his Guest Editorial in our May 1974 issue, the biological sciences have indeed reached the point where the results of research will soon have titanic influences on every human being on this planet. But a simple fear reaction, the kind that says, "There are some things man was not meant to tamper with, Dr. Frankenstein," is not only absurd, it is useless.

Last year, European physicians revealed that several "test-tube" human babies had been born successfully. Fertilized ova had been removed from donor mothers, incubated for a week or so in laboratory apparatus, and then re-implanted in the mothers' wombs. The fetuses developed normally and the babies were born naturally.

Also, a group of biological researchers bypassed the usual channels of scientific communication and called a public press conference to ask for a moratorium on research dealing with artificial genes. Appealing directly to the public (and to the Government: the press conference was held in Washington), they pointed out that research has now reached the point where artificial genetic material can be grafted onto the genes of bacteria, such as *Escherichia coli,* the microscopic guinea pig of most genetic researchers.

E. coli is an ubiquitous little fellow; one of his favorite habitats is the digestive tract of human beings. If the artificially mutated strains of *E. coli* that have been produced in laboratory experiments should ever get loose, the effect could be strange new diseases for which there is no cure. The scientists called for a halt to such research until adequate safeguards are drawn up and enforced.

So what happened? Most researchers announced they would go along with the moratorium until reasonable safeguards were put into effect. Most, but not all. Some researchers felt that their laboratories were already properly safeguarded, and they weren't going to halt their work because other people might be sloppy. There was no way to enforce the ban; it was strictly self-imposed and self-enforced.

Earlier this year, the biologists announced that they had produced a satisfactory set of regulations, and research could now go ahead. But the safeguards are *still* self-imposed and self-enforced; the scientific community is attempting to police itself in ways that the nuclear physicists attempted only after Hiroshima. The biologists are trying to prevent their Hiroshima from happening.

Certainly self-regulation by the scientists is preferable to Government regulation, in the view of the scientists themselves. Given the way the Government has handled the nuclear power situation, self-regulation may be infinitely preferable for all concerned.

But will it work? And what of all the other results that will be coming out of the biological research labs, and the behavioral research facilities, and the pharmaceutical laboratories? We have only seen the tip of the iceberg, so far; the biological sciences are now the "blue sky" areas of research. The vistas are almost limitless; the prospects for human improvement—and debasement—are staggering.

At this stage of the game, *only* imaginative and well-informed science fiction writers can accurately show the scope of future developments in the biological sciences. And the implications for the future of the human race. The scientists themselves can't do it; they're too close to the subject. The futurologists can't do it; they're constrained to accept only what the scientists tell them. But SF writers can absorb what is known, what is predicted by the experts, and add the "wild card" kind of thinking that goes beyond simple straightline extrapolation.

The biological sciences should be—*must* be—a "blue sky" area for science fiction, too. We need to look squarely and fairly at the possibilities coming out of the biological labs and show the world how they will affect the human race. Not simple-minded cloning stories, in which the writer hasn't the faintest idea of how cloning works and produces something akin to a 1940's Bela Lugosi movie script. Not stories with the moral short-sightedness of a "Do not tamper, Dr. Frankenstein" attitude. We need stories that examine *all* the implications, for good and evil, of current and projected biological research.

Consider: Test-tube babies will never replace the natural method of gestating humans. Really? How about the jet set, who don't want to be encumbered by unsightly pregnancies? Or women who are too physically frail to survive pregnancy and childbirth? Or "generation" type starships? Or in situations where the mother will surrender the child for adoption? Or . . . you get the idea.

Consider: The research on artificial genes that caused all the moratorium fuss has the potential not only of producing new human diseases and/or biological weapons. It can also be used to produce incredibly inexpensive medical drugs for healing. Or for making ordinary plants and bacteria nitrogen-fixers, so that our need for fertilizer drops astoundingly. Or for correcting human genetic disorders such as sickle-cell anemia or diabetes or ... take it from there.

Consider: If we solve our population growth problems and achieve a zero-growth situation at a total world population of, say, four to eight billions, genetic engineering will become *necessary* to the survival of the human race. In a zero-growth situation, the birthrate will be too low to allow normal genetic "competition" to erase genetic defects. The defectives will be born and will survive to breed more defectives. The genetic pool will degrade until there isn't a human being on the planet without defective genes. Genetic engineering can correct those defects when natural selection cannot.

Now consider that the words "defective genes" mean very different things to an Albert Schweitzer and an Adolf Hitler.

It's high time science fiction got busy playing its very important game in this very crucial area of scientific research.

New Worlds For Old

You have to blame my wife, Barbara, for this one. She was the one who brought Harris's book, *Cows, Pigs, Wars and Witches* into the house and got me to read it. I began by hating the snippets she had quoted to me. I ended by writing this Editorial in praise of his book and a couple of others that I liked equally well. I even touted Harris's book to Isaac Asimov. The publishing industry being as astute as it is, though, Isaac couldn't buy, borrow, or even steal the damned book. The publishers had let it go out of print a few months after they had put it on the market. (Why writers go gray.)

We like to tell each other that science fiction is *the* literature of ideas, and that science fiction people are always open to new concepts. "No future shock for us," we say, "because we realize that *change* is the most important factor in human experience."

True, up to a point. Unfortunately, sometimes our thinking gets into ruts. The bold new ideas we deal with become clichés eventually, and too often we like those ideas so well that we don't bother to update them or go out and develop new ones.

For example: Most science fiction stories about the future of space exploration and colonization assume that human settlements will be established on the Moon and Mars within the next half-century. Further outposts of humanity will be set up on Mercury, and the satellites of Jupiter and Saturn. Colonization of Venus will be impossible for a long time to come because of the planet's incredibly inhospitable surface conditions: choking carbon dioxide atmosphere as thick as overcooked chicken gumbo soup, and temperatures hot enough to melt aluminum.

Yet this overworked, predictable scenario was already out-of-date in the 1950's. It was obviously naive because no one had asked the basic questions: *Why* would any human society spend the money, time and effort necessary to colonize the Moon or another world? Where would the profit be for the people who pay the bills? (And also, how do you make a space transportation system efficient enough to carry colony-sized payloads?)

No nation, no corporation, no society is going to colonize

anyplace just to satisfy the predictions of science fiction writers. The Apollo project landed astronauts on the Moon not because Delos D. Harriman cajoled us into doing it, but because our political leaders found it expedient to demonstrate our technological superiority to the world.

More on that later. Let's take another example, this time from the social sciences. The future societies depicted in most science fiction stories are depressingly unimaginative. Interstellar empires (if you can believe that they could exist!) are modeled either on the Roman or British imperial systems. Smaller social units are portrayed either as some variation of feudalism, if they're backward; or modern American industrialism; or a totalitarian regime *à la* Nazi Germany or Soviet Russia. If a society's really backward, or just immature, we get a modern American's version of Paleolithic hunting tribes. Out of all the possibilities of human interactions, most science fiction writers cling to the tiny slice of European social structure that they learned (often incompletely) in public school.

Occasionally a writer will produce a story in which a human society is patterned after the social insects, or some other animal species. Usually these stories don't work out well because people don't think or behave like bees, termites, Thomson's gazelles, or turtledoves. Trying to squeeze human characters into the social patterns of an ant can get pretty ridiculous, unless the writer is trying to make an allegory. And it takes a very good writer to make a successful allegory.

When existing information is no longer sufficient for your purposes, the only sane thing to do is go out and get more information. Unfortunately, too many writers have fallen into the habit of depending on the "old reliable" ideas and information. In a universe of change, they continue to produce stories that are weary, stale, flat and unprofitable.

On the other hand, there's a world of ideas and information surrounding us. Despite political setbacks and funding woes, scientists are still thinking, investigating, studying, and producing the basic raw material for good, strong, vital, new science fiction stories.

Consider three books: *Cows, Pigs, Wars, and Witches: The Riddle of Culture,* by Marvin Harris (Random House); *The Third Industrial Revolution,* by G. Harry Stine (Putnam); and *Pioneer Odyssey, Encounter with a Giant,* by Richard O. Fimmel, William Swindell, and Eric Burgess (NASA SP-349).

Burgess and Stine are no strangers to *Analog*'s audience. But it is Harris's book that offers the most challenging new ideas (sorry, Harry and Eric). An anthropologist at Columbia University, Harris has set out to examine, in his own words, "The causes of apparently irrational and inexplicable life-styles." He goes on to say:

> Some of these enigmatic customs occur among preliterate or "primitive" peoples—for example, the boastful American Indian chiefs who burn their possessions to show how rich they are. Others belong to developing societies, my favorite being the Hindus who refuse to eat beef even though they're starving. Still others have to do with messiahs and witches who are part of the mainstream of our own civilizations. To make my point, I have deliberately chosen bizarre and controversial cases that seem like insoluble riddles.

His point is that even the most wildly inexplicable examples of human behavior can be understood as responses to the social, geophysical, and economic environment of the people involved. For example, Harris compares a Hindu's eating his "sacred cow" to an American's burning down the factory in which his farm machinery is made.

For science fiction people, Harris's book is a gem. The man goes in and investigates the way human societies *work.* He studies and prods beneath the surface of things, in an effort to find out why people behave the way they do. You may not agree with his conclusions in each case, but they will provide several banquets' worth of food for thought.

The lesson Harris has to teach science fiction writers is this: if we can understand the way existing and historic human societies have worked, then we can begin to understand how to construct future societies that are not merely copies of high school history texts.

The techniques Harris uses, and the way the man thinks, offer a primer to any writer who desires to construct valid and viable fictional societies, whether they be future variants of human societies on Earth, or alien societies set on other worlds. You start with the geophysical facts—the landscape, the climate, the natural resources—and build from that foundation a society that is ecologically fitted into its environmental niche.

Getting back to the colonization of the Solar System, it seems obvious that our first space colonies will not be on the Moon, or even in the Lagrangian orbital positions championed by Professor Gerard O'Neill and his Princeton cohorts. As G. Harry Stine pointed out in the January and February 1973 issues of this magazine, the first large-scale migration of human beings off-world won't go very far—a mere couple of hundred kilometers.

The Third Industrial Revolution makes a convincing case for the idea that we can—and should—begin to develop industrial factories in space. Far from being an inhospitable, difficult and dangerous environment, the zero-gravity world of factories in orbit around the Earth offers tremendous advantages over ground-based industrial operations.

The best of these advantages is the effect large-scale orbital industries could have on Earth itself. We can escape the inevitable doom of the "Limits to Growth" argument by tapping the natural resources of the entire Solar System, while at the same time moving most industrial operations off-planet and allowing our homeworld to become a clean, green, pleasant place to live in.

Unlike earlier predictions of space colonization, Stine's proposals make economic and social sense. You can see reasons for spending the money and effort to make the Third Industrial Revolution a reality. There is a profit motive for almost everyone on Earth, in the economic, political and even environmental sense. And with large-scale industrial operations in orbit, prospectors and miners will comb the Moon and the asteroids for metals and minerals: the Moon because it's the closest "mine" we have (closer, in energy costs, even than the Earth) and the asteroids because heavy metals are there and they can be transported Earthward by fairly simple and cheap methods, such as nuclear "shaped charges" that will provide enough thrust to nudge whole asteroids into orbits close to the Earth-Moon system.

Put Harris's book and Stine's together, and you can begin to draw marvelous scenarios about future human societies on Earth and in space. The variations are practically limitless.

For example: What happens to the Middle East when the Third Industrial Revolution makes the oil deposits there much less valuable than they are today? In a recent issue of *Science* magazine, a report spoke gloomily of the chances that the oil-producing nations can quickly convert their immense inflow of cash into a modern industrialized society. Saudi Arabia and Iran will still be backward and overpopulated with illiterates, the report concludes, because it takes many generations to develop the administrative and managerial skills necessary to run a modern industrialized nation.

Perhaps. But what if an international corporation goes into the business of "developing" new societies? Such a corporation could send a team of administrators, managers, and teachers to Iran, for instance, to begin the rapid buildup of that nation's industrial and economic base, while at the same time teaching the natives how to do the job. The corporation would have a contract with the Iranian government, the Shah would have his army to make sure that the corporation didn't try to become politically active. With modern administrative techniques, computers, electronic communications, and teaching techniques that are not hampered by academic fussiness, a nation like Iran might become administratively self-sufficient in a remarkably short time.

The key to such a scenario is the ability to work out new solutions to the problems being faced, rather than wringing your hands over the inability of the old solutions to get the job done. In 1941, just before the United States entered World War Two, every shipbuilder in the land *knew* it took four years to build a capital ship, such as an aircraft carrier. By late 1942, after a year of war, the US Navy had exactly two carriers left in the entire Pacific. By late

1944, the Navy had more than a hundred carriers. New ways of constructing them had been found, some of them ridiculously simple, such as working triple shifts.

Pioneer Odyssey is a thorough, and thoroughly beautiful, report on the Pioneer 10 spacecraft mission to Jupiter. Every aspect of the mission is shown in careful detail, from the original planning of the mission to the last-minute "interstellar cave painting" that was affixed to the spacecraft. Burgess and his co-authors have done a lovely job.

Now that we know so much more about Jupiter, we must all rethink the story possibilities of the giant planet. Jupiter's intense magnetosphere bathes its inner satellites with radiation that would be lethal to humans. Does that mean we can no longer deal with stories set on Io, Callisto, Ganymede or Europa? Or must we get inventive enough to find ways to allow human explorers and engineers to live and work in deadly radiation fields? Remember, water will be the most precious resource in the entire Solar System, off Earth, and it appears that the closest sure waterhole to us is Jupiter and its satellites.

Jupiter itself is a new world for us to explore in our stories. There's energy radiating up from below those surface clouds. There are complex chemical compounds in those clouds and perhaps biological activity below them. Can we ever explore Jupiter? And if we do, and we find living creatures there, how will we be able to determine if they're intelligent or not?

There are worlds within worlds, waiting for new human insights that will turn them into memorable science fiction stories. To cite from the dedication of *Pioneer Odyssey:*

> This book is dedicated to all the citizens of the United States of America who have made this program of interplanetary exploration possible and who, along with all mankind, will benefit from the increased awareness of the universe and how the Earth and its peoples relate to it.

Science fiction writers, please take notice!

Space: 1999, Marked Down From 2001

I was surprised and flattered when Hollis Alpert, of the American Film Institute, phoned me to ask for a review of the television SF series, *Space: 1999.* The review turned into a general polemic about why SF films turn out the way they do. The title came from a crack made by Mark Chartrand, director of the Hayden Planetarium in New York, who is a science fiction reader and good friend, as well as being a punster of the Spider Robinson class.

To paraphrase the late Fred Allen, you can stuff all the good science fiction films which have ever been made into a flea's navel and still have room for three pieces of lint and an agent's heart.

The latest science fiction execration to hit television, *Space: 1999,* is just another example of how producers can spend perfectly good money to achieve perfectly dreadful results. The moral of this tale: Spectacular special effects do not of themselves make a good film. There's much more to science fiction than blinking hardware and pyrotechnic explosions.

In fact, for most science fiction film productions, the quality of the work as a film is inversely proportional to the money spent on special effects. If you doubt this is true, go see *Rollerball.* The special effects are terrific. All the other aspects of the film are considerably less than terrific.

Why should this be? Why does a medium, which can recreate the Crimean War in faithful detail and explore the innermost passions of the human heart with exquisite artistry, fall so flat on its face almost every time it tackles science fiction?

The answer is simply that most filmmakers neither understand nor appreciate the particular strengths and problems science fiction offers. To begin with, science fiction is a literary form that has always appealed to a rather limited readership which enjoys cerebral exercise. Science fiction has been called the literature of change.

Commercial motion pictures are a mass-audience medium. The mass audience in the main wants to be entertained, not challenged or exercised cerebrally. They'd much rather see Fred Astaire dance than have him make concerned speeches about the responsibility of nuclear scientists for World War III, as he did in *On the Beach.*

For television, the problem gets worse. The purpose of commercial television is to capture the largest possible audience for the advertisers. Lowest common denominator and all that. Challenge assumptions? Make the audience think? Be interesting enough so that they'll talk to each other during commercials? Heresy!

All right, then. Science fiction as published in books and magazines is not a mass medium form of entertainment and probably never will be. But isn't there a middle ground where science fiction can be adapted for the mass audience? After all, the film industry has made commercial and artistic successes out of Shakespeare, Dickens, Tolstoy, and Hemingway. Why can't the enormous collection of talent among the filmmakers turn out good science fiction?

We must look deeper—into science fiction itself, and into the way most filmmakers approach a science fiction project.

At heart, science fiction is a form of storytelling in which the characters in the stories are powerfully affected by some sort of scientific discovery or new technological invention. Take away the science and technology and you have no story. Thus, *Frankenstein* is a science fiction novel dealing with the newfound ability of a scientist to create human life and of the consequences of that scientific breakthrough.

Science fiction writers have always been aware science can kill as well as cure. Verne. Wells. Asimov. Heinlein. Bradbury . . . right on through to the newest and freshest writers of today, they have all shown that science is a double-edged sword. Many stories show science and technology solving humanity's age-old problems of disease, poverty, and death. But many other stories show science causing new problems, and technology exacerbating the old ones.

The first major science fiction films, such as Fritz Lang's *Metropolis* (1926), dealt with the dehumanizing aspects of science and technology. That is what you would expect from the gloomy, disheartened era between World War I and II, especially from a Germany that was heading into Nazism. Another direction was exemplified by a European coproduction in the early thirties, *Transatlantic Tunnel* (1935). Despite guest appearances by Walter Huston and George Arliss, and a jut-jawed performance by Richard Dix, the main attractions of the film were the special effects: spectacular disasters deep beneath the ocean floor, gigantic machines pitted against underwater volcanoes, and all that.

It was a naive film. Its plot was sheer Victorian nonsense, with stiff-lipped heroes and their noble, long-suffering wives. Philosophically, the film was straight out of the gadget-happy, gee-whiz school of science fiction. We're building a tunnel under the Atlantic Ocean! Golly! Never mind that volcano, men, we'll bore right through it! Hang on! Here we go!

When the tunnel's finished, everybody shouts hurrah and the film ends, presumably with everyone happy.

It seemed clear to moviemakers that science fiction could be used in two basic ways, one for "deep" philosophical issues, the other for exotic adventures heavy on special effects, and with little else to recommend them. So we got high-budget bores such as *Things to Come* (1936) with H.G. Wells's message of "progress or stagnation, which shall it be?" The mass audience chose to ignore the issue, and the film. On the other hand, we got technically accurate (for its day) adventures such as *Destination Moon* (1950) with Robert A. Heinlein's message of "space is the new frontier . . . and it's fun!"

By the fifties, Hollywood was producing an occasional thoughtful science fiction film which blended good special effects with a good script. *The Day the Earth Stood Still* (1951) dealt with an alien visitor who warns the people of Earth to stop messing around with nuclear weapons or suffer total destruction.

But these noble few films were buried beneath garbage heaps of monster movies which were advertised as "sci-fi," a barbarism which still raises the hackles of science fiction fans. We were treated to a parade of teenaged werewolves, giant Gila monsters, Japanese foot stompers who regularly flattened Tokyo, enormous spiders, creatures from black lagoons who kept returning again and again, huge dung beetles, and alien invaders who came down in flying saucers to chase starlets across the desert.

Calling these monster movies sci-fi did more damage to real science fiction than Godzilla ever did to Tokyo.

The best science fiction film ever made was produced in Britain in 1951: Alexander Mackendrick's *The Man in the White Suit*, starring Alec Guinness. This film accomplished things that no science fiction film did before or since, depicting the sheer thrill of doing scientific research, the long hunt for a new scientific breakthrough, and the way a new scientific idea is often violently rejected by all the rest of the human race. It did all this with sparkling humor and a minimum of special effects.

How could this film be so good while most of the others are so bad? I suspect it was because Mackendrick, Guinness, and company had no idea they were making a science fiction film. They were making a movie. Period. Therefore, they paid careful attention to quality in the script, the acting, and the production values. Quite a contrast to the usual sci-fi formula of spending your money on spectacular special effects and letting the rest fall where it may.

By the sixties, television began to take up where feature films had left off. Not only did the old sci-fi flicks become a staple of late night masochism, but new series such as *Outer Limits, The Twilight Zone, Lost in Space,* and *The Time Tunnel* drove more dull wooden stakes into the heart of science fiction's reputation. Most of these shows quickly degenerated into monsters and nonsense. Only *Twilight Zone* maintained any semblance of taste and intelligence, but even there the shows were usually fantasy, whimsy, or supernatural horror. Few were truly science fiction.

All this was happening while science fiction novels and short stories were attracting new readers and facing social problems such as racism, overpopulation, and energy shortages decades before they made headlines. Science fiction was becoming respectable in the nation's universities. The old pulp magazine image of the lurid

Twenties and Thirties was finally being outgrown. But the movies and TV shows which called themselves science fiction were still solidly in the old "gee whiz" era.

That is, until the late Sixties, when Stanley Kubrick and Arthur C. Clarke combined forces to produce *2001: A Space Odyssey*. Visually one of the most stunning films ever made, it also had a powerful philosophical message—in fact, two of them.

The first, of course, is that our tools are taking control over us. From shinbone-turned-warclub to the soft-spoken, chess-playing electronic computer named Hal, all our tools are killers. The second, subtler message of *2001* is that the human race has been shaped and manipulated by entities from outer space who are far older and wiser than we. Why and how they changed us from apes to men is unknown. But they did it. And now they have changed one human astronaut into something new, a Star Child, who returns to Earth for who knows what purposes.

2001 was a "message" film with incredibly good special effects. But it became enormously popular not for its message(s)—which confused hell out of the mass audience—but for its psychedelic "light show" toward the end of the film. Kids of all ages toked up and took in the show, pleasantly buzzed, ignoring the philosophy while they watched the pretty lights and listened to the electronic music. It was a triumph of the audience's ignorance over the filmmaker's intelligence.

The film studios saw it as a triumph of special effects, and a spate of science fiction films and TV specials were rushed into production. Most of them were dismal, and the one directed by Douglas Trumbull—who had done the special effects for *2001*—was the most dismal of them all. Trumbull's *Silent Running* (1972) had good special effects, but little else. It had the philosophical depth of a freshman debate, the scientific accuracy of a medieval sorcerer, and the dramatic power of a penlight battery.

Television's *Star Trek* series came the closest to doing

consistently good science fiction. Many of the scripts were not only intelligent, but interesting. The series' main characters were lively and almost believable. All this was due to the vision and perseverance of Gene Roddenberry, the show's creator and executive producer. Roddenberry knows and likes science fiction, and he got several science fiction writers to help make *Star Trek* a success.

But the fanatical audience which *Star Trek* attracted, and still holds even though the show has been off the air for years except as reruns, was due only in small part to its excellence as science fiction. The core of *Star Trek*'s fandom consists of adolescents and retarded postadolescents called "Trekkies"—who are turned on by the character Spock, a half-human, half-alien, tall, and taciturn male who is unemotional, enormously competent, and totally unavailable. The ultimate father figure. Many of the Trekkies have grown up and become mothers and fathers, but it's still Spock, with his pointy ears and deadpan brilliance, for whom they pine.

Which brings us to *Space: 1999*. A science fiction film buff remarked that the title for this show should be "*Space: 1999, Marked Down from 2001.*"

The influence of the Kubrick/Clarke film is obvious throughout *1999*: the astronomical shots, the stylish hardware, the pretentious musical background, and the cast's stiff-faced, witless dialogues. But while Kubrick was trying to make a point with his wooden actors, *1999* merely has wooden actors. And actresses. Barbara Bain looks as if she's just stumbled out of electroshock therapy (although her hair is nicely done); Martin Landau seems to have a chip on his shoulder. Probably he's wondering how he ever let himself get talked into such inanities.

For while Kubrick had in Arthur C. Clarke one of the best and most knowledgeable science fiction writers in the world, *1999* has no informed scientific input whatsoever. And although most film and TV producers don't like to admit it, it is the scientific content of science fiction that sets it apart from other forms of drama. It is inevitable, moreover, that a production in which the science is sluffed off will be a production in which everything else gets sluffed off, sooner or later. Quality is a quantum effect; you either pay attention to it or you don't.

I speak from bitter experience. For six months I was the science advisor on the worst science fiction TV series ever produced: *The Starlost.* As drama, it rated a few light-years below watching grass grow. As science fiction, it was filled with so many idiocies that I gave up and withdrew from the series.

A science advisor's task is to read the scripts, in first draft preferably, and point out the scientific errors in them. All in the interest of scientific accuracy. A good science advisor also suggests ways to correct the errors without bending the script out of shape. I was well paid by *The Starlost* production, thanked profusely for catching ludicrous errors, praised for my team spirit when I showed how to work around such infelicities. And then ignored. The scripts were shot exactly as originally written, errors and all.

If the scientific gaffes were the only problems with *The Starlost* series, one might be tempted to forego severe criticism. But the producers' attitude toward scientific niceties ("Don't worry about it; nobody will notice") carried over into all the other facets of the series. They didn't worry about the quality of the story ideas or of the scripts. They didn't worry about the cheap-jack sets and props, or the incredibly bad acting and directing. As a result the shows were unbelievably dull, as well as stupid. The series quickly folded.

Space: 1999 appears to be heading for success, not collapse. But I wonder how long a sizable audience can be kept interested in bad acting, poor scripts, and absurd situations? Acting and dramatic impact are qualities any audience can judge for itself, and certainly *1999* will win no awards in those categories. What seems to be selling the show is its "science fictional" appeal: the blinking hardware and spectacular special effects.

But it will take more than special effects to keep the show

going. As science fiction, *Space: 1999* is awful. There are no challenging ideas, and the scientific aspects of the show are sheer *lunarcy.*

Consider: The original premise of the show is that the moon is blasted out of its orbit by the explosion of radioactive wastes, which have been stored on the moon so that they cannot contaminate Earth's ecology.

Radioactive wastes can't explode. They're *wastes.* Most of the energy has been taken out of them already. They are radioactive, and therefore dangerous, but no more likely to explode than the cooling ashes of a wood fire are apt to spontaneously burst into flame.

Somehow the radiation from these stored nuclear wastes affects the mentality of the lunar workers. Mysteriously, while Barbara Bain looks at them over closed-circuit television, they go insane. No explanation.

Not only is this lousy science, this entire miasmic concept plays up to the public's fear of nuclear energy and makes it just that much harder to convince people in the real world that nuclear energy is a reasonable alternative to Middle Eastern oil.

All right. Back to *1999.* The stuff explodes and acts like a huge rocket thruster, pushing the moon with incredible fury out of its orbit and away from Earth. Or so we're told.

The explosion effects are impressive, although clearly those explosions are taking place in an earthly studio, not on the airless moon. Without air there is no sound. Compare the televised takeoff of the Apollo lunar modules from the moon's surface, and you will see the differences immediately. The basic idea of knocking the moon out of its orbit just doesn't stand up to examination.

The moon is a massive chunk of rock. Its mass is about eighty million trillion tons. That's an eight with nineteen zeroes after it. To push it out of its orbit would take a nuclear explosion of many millions of megatons, at least. And an explosion of that force would shatter the moon completely. The moon is made out of fairly rigid rock, not green cheese. An explosion of that magnitude would destroy it.

It's an astronomical Catch 22. You need millions of megatons of explosive force to push the moon out of its orbit. But an explosion that size would be too strong for the moon to withstand. It would be shattered into billions of fragments. No more moon. No more life on Earth, very likely, after all the pieces finished raining down on us. Certainly no more *Space: 1999.*

But mere physics and astronomy don't deter sci-fi filmmakers. The moon hurtles out of its orbit into the mysterious depths of interstellar space it journeys. And once a week it manages to stop at some strange new planet and have an adventure.

Now *Star Trek*'s spaceship, the "U.S.S. Enterprise," could visit a new planet every week because it had engines, navigators, and a crew aboard. But a runaway moon just doesn't seem likely to roll by a planet on a weekly schedule, stop and loiter in the vicinity for a while, and then roll blithely onward as the final commercials fill the screen. It strains one's credulity.

What's more, we are told in the second segment of the series that the moon has been journeying for several months, and has now reached the edge of the galaxy. "Galaxy" is a word sci-fi filmmakers seem to prefer above all other astronomical terms. Maybe it's because the word sounds intriguing and mysterious to them. Certainly they have no concept of what a galaxy is.

Our galaxy is the Milky Way, a titanic collection of about a hundred billion stars, of which our own sun is one. At the speed that *1999*'s moon is traveling, it would take a hundred million years to reach the nearest edge of our galaxy. It may seem as though a hundred million years passes during every boring segment of *Space: 1999,* but the scripts say otherwise.

Why go on? The show is *dumb.* The science is utter nonsense. The scripts are bogging down into monsters and weirdos in outer space. And the producers are apparently uttering the same, "Don't worry about it; nobody will notice," which has doomed so many science fiction projects in the past.

And this is the fundamental reason for so much bad science fiction in films and on television. As long as the special effects are eye-catching (and in many cases, even when they aren't) the producers don't give a damn about anything else.

The audiences notice these things, often much sooner than the producers expect. A show based on special effects and monsters quickly pales before the eyes of even the least critical viewer. The shame of it is that people who might honestly be attracted to the exciting, thought-provoking worlds of good science fiction will take a look at *Space: 1999* and go back to watching reruns of Lucy.

And who can blame them?